To: Mandy &

For Strength   e

MW01123043

Alberta Mann

Inc

BREAKING FREE

Alberta Mann

authorHOUSE®

AuthorHouse™
1663 Liberty Drive
Bloomington, IN 47403
www.authorhouse.com
Phone: 1 (800) 839-8640

Published by AuthorHouse 08/27/2015

ISBN: 978-1-5049-2941-7 (sc)
ISBN: 978-1-5049-3220-2 (e)

Print information available on the last page.

Any people depicted in stock imagery provided by Thinkstock are models,
and such images are being used for illustrative purposes only.
Certain stock imagery © Thinkstock.

This book is printed on acid-free paper.

Because of the dynamic nature of the Internet, any web addresses or links contained in
this book may have changed since publication and may no longer be valid. The views
expressed in this work are solely those of the author and do not necessarily reflect the
views of the publisher, and the publisher hereby disclaims any responsibility for them.

Dedicated to: Mom

Heavenly Father must have known that I needed you for my mom. I am grateful to have been chosen to be one of your daughters.

I knew you were not there in that hospital room. I could not feel your essence. You had gone on to the next step of your journey.

I remember the snow fell softly all that day, mixed with sunlight. It continued to fall steadily as we drove through the night.

A blanket of white spread across the fields and hills, caught on tree branches bare, swirled in breezes, filled the air.

The roads were thick with it, Beautiful, Unmarked, Pure. The World grew Quiet, Muted, Peaceful, Still.

And into this Place and this Night … God came quietly, reached out His Hands, Gathered you Gently in Loving Arms and Carried you safely HOME.

You needed to go.

We thought we were too late, but the Secret of Love is …. "It Waits".

I know Mom is waiting for us now and "Fear Not", Mom will still be directing our footsteps here below, from up above.

In countless ways when we need to make choices, hers will be the voice we hear. Around every corner, the memories will come. They equal Love.

A clear running stream backed by sumac will remind us of Home. Roast beef done to perfection and strawberry rhubarb pie.

Mom at the end of a broom chasing racoons off the balcony and placing muffins on the clothes line for the squirrels.

I will be watching more baseball games because she loved them. She was like Chinese food, both sweet and sour, the combination irresistible.

I am looking at the faces of your family Mom. They are beautiful, individual, unique, precious.

Into each life you have, stretched their minds, opened their hearts, shown them strength, pushed them to follow their dreams, shaped and moulded.

This may not be the picture that you could have painted, if given the time, but they are your Masterpiece Mom, your Life's Work. Well done!

You could have given me no greater Gift, than this Family.

"There are countless stars that shine on high and other worlds, beyond our eyes, but here on Earth, we live by Faith and Search for Truth.

Always there are those that God has set apart. They walk with Strength, Courage and Purity of Heart.

They put their hand in the "Hand of God' holding firm to the "Iron Rod." They are the Soldiers, which walk, Unchallenged, Humbly, Unto Glory.

Mom you are one of them, and I Love you."

No words can ever express my thankfulness for all the love you bestowed upon me and my children.

(smc)

CHAPTER 1

<u>**(Tracking one woman's journey)**</u>

<u>**The Human Condition:**</u>

"We get hit, we get back up. We are knocked down and we stumble to our feet. A door closes and we search for a window with light."

Come walk with me. Let the words travel uncensored through your mind. Open your heart. Turn the pages, one by one. Follow the unexpected twists and turns. There will be valleys low and mountains high, shadows and light, emotions deep and true, frailty and a strength never failing. Trust will be lost by actions that destroy lives. Understanding, anger and compassion will be found and accepted. Through great sadness the desire and freedom to fly free will be possible. Through each step, every choice, all lessons, (like a butterfly discovering its wings) the knowledge of **"who am I really?"** still exists.

Never for one moment, forget this. Know that endings are only beginnings, **"beginnings without end!"** It's called the "Human Condition" and we could not exist without this.

And so here I am. As the saying goes …. "When I was a child, I thought as a child." As a young girl I believed in all things beautiful. Life was simpler then. I was conceived in Love, raised in Love, surrounded by Love. Love was all that I knew. I was Happy!

One day at the tender age of 37, I woke to something called, **"Reality".** That reality would now be my world. The safety net was stripped away and I was falling. My husband of 18 years, the man that I adored, turned and walked away. There had been no warning, he gave no reason, we had no protection, from such a selfish act.

I believe now, that he was lost. Years and years and years later, I came to understand that for him, he was only doing, **"the best I can."** That it was not near enough is an understatement in futility. I do believe that he never knew the destruction that he had left behind. I would like to believe that if he knew, he would not wish to survive this knowledge. That is something known as hope, for the man that I once loved.

The very fabric of my life lay in shreds, beyond repair. I never knew there could be so much pain. Like a fawn frozen in the lights of an oncoming locomotive, I barely had time to leap out of the way. I carried the pain with me. I thought it would kill me. For just a second, I welcomed it. The coward within that I never knew existed, was rattling my cage. I refused to answer.

Beyond pain is where I travelled and quickly. There was much that I had to do. My children needed me. I was all that they had. Shoving my pain into the darkest corner of my mind and locking that door, firmly behind me, I gathered my three young children into my arms and battled through the storm. Overnight, they had become, my children. Loving them I understood their confusion, pain, fear. As their Mom, I could never allow them, to see mine.

They needed to know that I was strong. Strength is what I gave them. They needed me to love them and so I loved them more than ever before. They would need a new home, shelter, protection and Hope. I worked towards all of this. Their need to Trust in someone was magnified. I gave them me. Was that enough? I just wanted them to be happy.

Hopefully my children never knew how scared I really was. Each time I saw and felt their pain, mine grew. Talk about mistakes, I made quite a few. I never meant to. From the darkness that had invaded our world, we travelled slowly towards the light. With no road map to follow and only the will to survive and protect my children, somehow I muddled through. No one ever said, **"Life would be easy."**

Over time, with blind Faith, a Strength never ending and family and friends, step by step we pushed through to a new world of endless possibilities. They say you need to play the hand you are dealt and it's how that hand is played that determines the ultimate quality of your life. I have been truly blessed.

Surprisingly I discovered that I would not have wanted to miss this journey, the journey that I didn't want to make. I have learned many things and am still learning. It's a source of ultimate joy. I am proud of and will always love my children. My grandchildren equal … **more Joy, intense Joy!**

My perspective on life and living has changed greatly. I love who I am. I will be true to me. I have expectations only of myself now. To all others, do the best you can. Remember never stop believing. Life is a Gift, Love is a Gift, and Time is a Gift. Concentrate most of all on, **'who am I really?'**

The answer to that question ….. lies within you …Life is a journey, (yours). Embrace it and be happy.

I grew up with the image of a husband and a father before me. Once I thought I had chosen such a man.

The Measure Of A Man

There is a standard by which I measure every man I meet.
He stands five foot nine inches. His hair is snow white. He
weighs in at approximately 160 lbs. His smile is sweeter than
honey, his heart pure as gold, his nature gentle and sunny.
He is a giver not a taker, how rare. I have never
known him to be the least bit unfair.
Sincerity, honesty, integrity, these are the things that come
naturally to him. He looks always for the good and more times
than not finds what others fail to see. He is a worker, a dreamer, an
engineering genius, shrouded in a cloak of humility, not prideful
about his accomplishments but rather, excited by them. The Spirit
that motivates him is unquenchable, his Faith, never failing.
He can lift a heavy load in his arms as easily as he holds with love, a
small child. He understands what Love is all about. He is my Dad.
He taught me to believe in myself, against all odds, however rough
the road. He taught by example, tempered always with love and
complete acceptance. His strength was unfailing and he never
stayed down, so neither can I. I want him to be proud of me.
Man can achieve greatness only when he comes to understand
and remember all that he has been given. It is with humility
that we accept our imperfections and it is with Faith that we
overcome them. My Dad is the greatest man I know.
He is the standard by which I measure, every man
I meet. It's hard to compete….. (smc)

CHAPTER 2

Bursting Bubbles

I'm in a battle field with fires burning. Smoke is blinding my eyes or is it tears that have dried? Bridges are destroyed, communication lost, children crying! Are they mine?

The world is spinning and I am hanging desperately at the top, fighting for control. I am shell shocked. My husband is missing in action! But wait, I see him in the distance or is that a stranger there, climbing out of this hell pit and walking away, intact, unscathed, not brave?

<u>Broken</u>

Little lady, crazy baby or broken doll.
Rules, Ethics, Morals do they mean, anything at all?
The Pallet lays smeared with life's muck, the
Artists' hand is frozen, stuck.
Inspiration stayed, the picture unfinished, its' clarity, frayed.
Upon the canvas the face is plain, etched with pain.
Drops of tears, stop sharply on the unfinished page.
The eyes are confused, hurt, dim,
Like a candle whose light is fading, from fighting the storms within.
Her grasp on reality is tunnelled to this time, this place.
She dangles at the top of the world, holding tight
With two tiny hands, the knuckles, stark, white.
Grasping an axel, rusted and cracked, swaying
earthbound and swinging back.
Her body floats, weightless, in fathomless space.
There is no time, has she run her last race?
Soft lips tremble, upon silent screams that go on forever.
Like a broken doll, beyond recall, she awaits the end.
Her last Prayer, **to feel nothing at all.**
A little lady, crazy baby or broken doll.
The picture is incomplete, yet the picture says it all. (smc)

Each day I walked with Fear stalking my every step and a pain so great I believed the weight of it would bury me.

This is a story about tremendous loss and unexpected treasures found. It is a journey of survival and renewal, one made with Hope, tremendous Faith, Limitless Courage and unexplored Strength. Through it all was a loving heart that refused to die.

In the eye of the storm struggling towards the sunlight a mother and her children break free.

I believe that some of you may have travelled the roads that I travelled. We may have passed along the way, each one of us at a different stage, coming from different backgrounds, carrying different tools, talents and beliefs.

There is Life after Charlie, Bob, Jane, Heather or whoever. There is Hope and a far better tomorrow than you can ever imagine right now.

The best part is, they do not get to dictate what we ourselves can become. We will not allow them, that Power! It is our Right to decide our own fate. Our choices that will bring this about. If you are at the beginning of this journey, I promise you, the **"Pain"** will end, the **"Fear"** will become your greatest Strength, the **"Anger"** will dissipate. You will walk forward from darkness into the Light and embrace **Joy!**

At the end of this journey that none of us wanted to make you will discover someone who is beautiful. That someone will be you. Trust me! Know that you are not alone, for others travel with you.

Bubbles bursting, pop, pop, pop! This story is true, oft repeated, sad and yet full of hope. I have started and stopped this book many times over the last two decades and yet, for the last six months I have felt a pressing need to get serious and ask time to stand still just for a moment, until I can get this down. Why now? I have no clear idea, but this will be it. Good, bad or indifferent, it will be wherever the keys of my computer take me.

As you struggle to survive the insanity that has taken hold of your soul, you will come to appreciate that this journey we didn't want to make, takes us upon a path of Survival and Discovery that we realize, we would not have wanted to miss. Unbelievable but true. Again, Trust me. I only wish there had been someone who understood, to walk through my hell with me.

<u>Life Begins And Ends With The Voice Within</u>

The voice within, grows strong, grows dim, it is saying,
"Are you listening?"
I choose not to travel all the roads unknown that lay before me,
Without a sense of self.
Without that knowledge, I am lost forever, on a path that leads to,
Nowhere I wish to be.
There is a purpose for this journey of hills,
valleys, forest, plains, darkness & light.
I will find it and at the end I believe ….. I will know joy.
I am always searching for knowledge to be gained,
Yet there is one thing constant, never changing ….
Truth remains.
I would not survive one day without it. (smc)

On November 23, 2014 I began again. The title was, 'The Human Condition.' I rather liked that title. I even finished it. It was short and sweet and very clear. Perhaps I should have stopped there, who knows.

At the age of 37, I believed I was old. If I had only known how crazy that thought was. I am now the amazing age of 65, retired and honestly can say I have never been bored. The world is too spectacular to ignore and I was much too busy not to embrace it. I write what I feel, what I feel is who I am. I have been where you may be standing now and my heart travels with you.

<u>Beyond Pain</u>

Beyond pain, that is where I have travelled, to a land devoid of hope,
A no man's world between reality and what might have been.
The burden of sadness lies heavy, upon a heart that cannot feel.
Only my memories are real.
So close to happiness, I touched it … Helpless, I watched it disappear.
I walked in chains, beyond pain, sentenced to a life I did not choose.
One forever, without you.
I stumbled to a hell where sadness reigns.
I cannot see the stars up in the heavens,
Or dawn breaking on a sea of blue.
The only thing my Heart can see,
Are memories of a world once shared by two.
They say we choose our own lives.
I refuse to believe those lies.
Now I walk in a world, devoid of hope …. Beyond Pain! (smc)

Often I feel like a traveller in a strange land without a road map or compass to guide me.

There are distractions that lure me on paths that I do not want to walk, yet sometimes you will find me there, lost, scared, alone and lonely, facing endless challenges and totally unprepared.

I had a husband I adored, 3 beautiful, happy children, a job I loved, a home I was proud of and quite frankly the world was mine. I was happy! I was a Fool!

CHAPTER 3

Life shatters at the most unexpected times and my world came tumbling down without warning. I was engulfed in a nightmare that remained upon awakening and for the first time in my Life ... I Knew Fear. The pain was incredible and I physically wanted to die, yet something stronger than self, held me back. It was my children. I needed to live for them. A long time later, I was still a mess, still floundering, still confused and making mistakes. Fortunately there were rays of sunlight through clouds of grey showing up intermittently throughout my days, but mostly I remained in the eye of the storm, searching for Hope.

Below is an actual experience bringing light and hope, into my life. Communing with nature always lifts my soul.

Ocean's Door

I stood at the edge of the world it seems,
Alone under God's Heaven,
And the night came in silently.
The sand shifted beneath my feet,
Running to meet the waves retreat.
The breeze was soft and sweet against my cheek,
And the only voice to split the night,
Came from the pounding on the Ocean floor.
Nice and slow, again and again and once more.
It was a scene of continuity,
And I sat upon the shore, until the darkness was no more.
And the night was replaced by the Miracle of Sunlight.
In the warmth of the sun's rays,
I raised my head in Praise,
For within the Peace that silenced me,
I could clearly see ...... Eternity. (smc)

I was in shock. I cannot begin to explain the Explosion of Pain, the Suffocating sense of Loss, the Bewilderment of Betrayal and the Terrifying reality of "Fear". I never saw it coming!

Apparently neither did our friends or co- workers. I was told that the people around us started paying close attention to their marriages. I had always believed it would never happen to me. I had thought that if you loved enough, nothing could go wrong.

I was so very wrong about that. Sometimes, love is not enough. Who knew?

I used to look at the couples whose marriages had broken down and think that they must have done something wrong, somewhere. Again I could not have been more wrong.

What a totally stupid, ridiculous judgment. I was oblivious to their suffering.

I will always be sorry for my lack of understanding. How dare I even offer an opinion on something so serious, so vital, when I had known absolutely nothing about it.

There is a saying, "sometimes Life happens while you are busy making other plans." Surprise!

In reality all we really have for sure is ourselves and that includes a body, a mind, a heart and endless possibilities. Life offers no guarantees. We are the masters of our own destinies. By the choices that we make, by our reactions to situations that we face, by our biased or unbiased understanding and comprehension at any given time, we will move forward or backward or stand still, frozen in time.

Ultimately, there is no one else to blame for the state that we are in, for all the choices that come after the initial impact of any storm, those choices are ours alone.

Reality struck hard and fast. I was in the real world. No more dreams of what might have been, no more happiness ever after. The little girl who dreamed of forever and always had grown into a woman and mother with something called Responsibility, and all the responsibility was mine.

I had never known emotional pain. I was drowning in it.

To face this new world of mine I planted a wooden smile upon my face as if nothing was wrong. Somewhere you find the strength.

Your best friends however can see past the walls of defenses you raise and one said to me, "we are in the ring, ducking and diving." I could picture us doing just that and fighting on the same team. She added, "I don't care if you come out with your eyes closed, just come out swinging!" Life has humor in it and laughter is one of the great healers.

My team was making a statement. I was not alone. Thank God

Wooden Smile

She walks through the crowd and she walks proud,
Head thrown back, shoulders straight with her womanly gait.
She catches the eye as she walks by.
Plastered in place on a near perfect face … she wears a wooden smile.
It leaves no trace of where she has been, the why, the how.
She does not laugh, she cannot win,
Her eyes do not reflect, that wooden grin.
They carry sadness and regrets, from deep within.
The woman walks alone, swallowed by the crowd,
Wanting to go home, but it's not allowed.
So she walks away, wearing her wooden smile… (smc)

This will be a very different book from the one I would have written at the beginning, regarding my personal nightmare, yet from a distance of 27 years everything has changed. Understanding and perspective and even compassion have been added and I feel sorry for the man that had it all and callously, without thought, walked away from his family. To this day I doubt he even realizes all that he has lost and how great, to those remaining, was the cost.

I am no longer young and foolish or delusional. At the age of 65 I am now a bonafide senior. The innocence that I once had, disappeared long ago and I will never be quite the same, not ever again, nor do I wish to be. Like a caterpillar that morphed into a butterfly I have experienced tremendous growth and knowledge which has carried me to, "safe harbour home." Now I spread my wings, catch the wind and fly wherever my heart desires. Free and Unfettered. Where does this incredible confidence come from? Well there is much to be said for sweet beginnings.

As a child, my life was built on a firm foundation of Love and Acceptance and a Sure Strong Faith. There were no put downs, not ever. Although we were not wealthy by anyone's standards we were rich in countless simple ways that matter. We were a happy and united family. Thankfully we still are today. We pull together when family is threatened. On matters of great import we stand firm. Love of family taught me always to hold onto a sense of self. I manage to do so, even now.

The following poem was written to my Father during the last year of his life in 2014. I think I need to tell you here, that during all the days of learning, my Father was the standard by which all men were measured. He was a simple man with an incredible life.

Daddy

Can you hear me, are you listening?
When I was just a little girl, you were my whole world.
You told me then, that I was the sweetest little girl in all the world.
Your love planted my feet, firmly on a path that has led me to here,
An adult grown with children and grandchildren of my own.
The journey was not anything that I expected,
nor as beautiful as I wanted.
Like the roller coasters that in later years you made,
My life became a series of ups and downs, with unexpected twists.
There was great joy in simple living and often tremendous pain.
I learned that we hurt in direct proportion to our capacity to love.
I never let go of the knowledge that you
instilled in me. I was beautiful.
There is a beauty deep inside that others may
not see, yet time will not erase.
We are the keepers of the Hearts, God gave to us ….
To use this Gift, is our greatest strength.
So while living to the fullest, my unpredictable life,
I go forward, without fear.
I search out Hearts I meet along the way,
Gather them to me, and here they stay.
These jewels so seldom seen … so often misunderstood,
Are precious Pools of Light, In a World gone crazy.
Daddy thank you for helping me to understand …..
The most important Gift from you,
Is to know who I am!
Daddy, can you hear me, are you listening?
I have loved you all of my life …and now
miraculously …. I love you more. (smc)

CHAPTER 4

When I was young I believed that Love was the most powerful thing in the world and for the record, I still believe it to be true. Love does not always make us happy but, if you have a heart, nothing else will do. Your search, when you are ready, must be only for a love that is deserving of you. There is no other possible choice.

Another fact learned over time, no one is allowed to treat you badly. End of story.

If we do not go around treating others badly, not even our enemies, then we must not accept bad behaviour from anybody else. Not family, not friends and especially not strangers. Stand firm on this. It's my bottom line. Just so you know. We matter.

In 1984, prior to my break up, I signed up for the Christopher Leadership Course at my old high school. It was fun and interesting and for graduation we each had to write and deliver a speech. Here is mine.

Chairperson, Fellow Christophers, Family and Friends.

Listen, have you heard? There is a power shortage, an energy crisis, and I say to you, Humbug! Eleven short weeks ago I joined a public speaking course. I was going to be a great orator and I learned something entirely different.

I watched a man large in stature and fair of face and he stood before us humbly, and I thought, **"How great you are."** I saw a young girl, exceedingly fair, with a shyness so great I could not comprehend it. She was like a lily of the valley, beautiful, yet overshadowed by the garden, and I watched her blossom like the rose. Young men stood before us of an age to have been my sons and they were proud and strong and I felt no fear for my future. And I watched a young mother. She was pretty, bright and gay, with eyes so clear and a smile so merry that she chased the shadows away.

I will never be a great orator. My talents must lie somewhere else and I will find them, but I could become a great person.

There is no one having known any of you that could doubt the greatness that is within us all. That power and strength that comes from within. We lit one candle in a darkened room and from it one more and one more, till the darkness was dispelled. We reached the inner person.

Ours is the Capacity to love. That Love should be the Power that moves our World. Think of the possibilities. There is no "Power Shortage." There is not one of you here that in your own special way, could not reach out and touch the life of someone and make a difference. I say to you, "Let your love so shine that the darkness no longer holds fear." (smc)

After my speech I was approached by teachers of the Course and asked if they could use my talk for their teachings. I was 35 years old, my life was before me and I was happy.

Three years later in the summer of 1987 tragedy struck. Betrayal was huge. Fear was a constant. My children were confused and hurting and not feeling safe as their world crumbled about them. There was little I could do to diffuse it. My husband was in control and no one knew exactly what he would do. I loved him and at that time I believed that I always would. Not so! Just to let you know, eventually I discovered that love dies or changes to something different or becomes … indifference. Thank God.

Just a warning. I will continue to get sidetracked but I want you to know that I know how important this is. I know that TRUST once lost is a very fragile commodity. I know now that TRUST must be earned. There is still a small part of me today that refuses to TRUST entirely. That is how Fragile, Trust can be. I wish it were not so.

<u>Love Died</u>

Love died, I think it died. This beautiful feeling deep inside,
Dried up and died. I didn't even see it go,
Until one morning I awoke and knew that it was so.
Love died ever so slowly. With every tear I cried,
Through all the pain I tried to hide.
Was it your total thoughtlessness to everything I represent?
The underlying coldness that was present?
The taking of all I had to give .. that did not allow .. love to live?
Love died. How could it possibly survive,
When every act of Love I gave to you, you twisted and denied,
Until the tenderness within, was cut to tiny ribbons?
Love died and I didn't see it go,
Until one morning I awoke and knew that it was so.
There are no tears left to cry, no need left to say Goodbye.
No reason to hold this pain within. Love died because it was denied,
And that's the greatest sin. ... For Love is Everything! (smc)

I have come to believe that we are the sum total of all the experiences, all the choices, all the challenges, all the happiness and all the pain. Life itself becomes the fabric of who we are and if we are brave enough to embrace it, it will enrich our lives.

Down the road of broken dreams, I walk, remembering. It was my 38th birthday and the year was 1987. We had been married for 18 years that summer, with the big house and the cushy jobs and three beautiful children.

The marriage did not last. Life happened somehow to take an unexpected turn and toppled us into our own private nightmare. My husband walked away unscathed to start a new life with a new family.

I was left with all the pieces of our lives held tightly in trembling hands.

Fumbling in the darkness that had become my life I searched for strength and with love I stood in the midst of the charred ruins of a life once lived, gathered my babies into my arms and began to fight the insanity that threatened to destroy all that remained of all those that I loved.

Where and why had daddy gone? Once there were 5 who lived, loved, laughed and worked together. Now there were 4 scrambling for a foothold.

With the Gift of time and distance I realized it's called**, "The human condition."** There is a little word **"why".** I have always asked this question my whole life through. It can equal clarity and bring understanding to a searching heart.

Do not be afraid to ask it of yourself. Trust the answers you discover. **Truth is there.** Your Truth.

CHAPTER 5

The End Began Like This:

Summer is upon us. I am happy and I love my family. My husband is the best man in the whole world, (I truly believed this) and we have three young beautiful children aged 14, 11, and 8. A year prior nearly to the day, we bought this wonderful new home. It was to be our, forever home. At the same time we invested in a new business. I had always loved and supported my husband in every dream he ever had and at this time, he had left his employer of many years and branched out into a business of his own. It was a huge, risky and exciting undertaking. Our life was busy and full. I had an amazing job in real estate at this time selling new homes, in a great area with few hours, which enabled me to help with the new business. I filled in where and when needed. Life was good.

Our new home had increased in value in that first year to the amount of approximately $100,000.00. We had known that the investment was good. This equity helped to keep the new business afloat for quite a long time. It was summer vacation and my husband said he could not take time away from the business. Since April he had been acting a little funny, not talking, seemingly lost in a world of his own. It was strange, unlike him. He had put me at a distance. I believed that he was worried about the office and his staff and loaded down with all the responsibility. He had borrowed quite heavily against the equity in our home. I believed he would come about. I believed in him. It turned out that I was an idiot to so believe.

The children and I went camping. It was our first trip alone without him. We had not been in touch while I was away and that in itself was strange. When I called in the evenings he didn't answer and I began to realize that something was terribly wrong. Where was he? I cut our vacation short and drove home unexpectedly. Instead of parking in our huge driveway, I left the car packed and parked up the street away from the house. To this day I am uncertain why I felt the need to do this. Intuition?

My husband came home and was surprised to find us there. Everything seemed normal. I made supper and we were eating when the doorbell rang. I was not expecting anyone and went to answer it. Standing on my front porch was a young blonde girl with blue eyes. I did not know her and she asked to speak to my husband. I left her standing outside.

It was then that I knew! I went to get him and left them at the door alone. He came back a few minutes later saying she worked with him and had some pictures she had wanted him to see. I wondered then how had she known where to find him. Perhaps our life would have remained in place if only she had been aware, that I had come home. Perhaps she would not have come! Or perhaps not. Who really knows?

NOTE: just so you know the vultures waiting outside our field of vision, (male or female) are prepared to take without conscience, plundering and destroying anything or anyone that gets in their way. The susceptible, the weak, the insecure, have no vision with which to see this. (My husband unfortunately, was one of these.)

I do know that he had not expected her, so whatever this was, it was relatively new. Of course we talked then, finally, my husband and I. There were no more strange silences. My husband was confused. I do know this to be true, for I could see it. Honest.

We tried in vain to figure this out but we really didn't have a clue. Now pain was all that I knew. We stayed together for perhaps a month during which time I was silently going insane, holding everything within while trying to spare my children, and dying inside a little more each day. The walls of my life were crashing in around me.

<u>Tears</u>

I could not let you see the tears I cried, I was too old to cry,
And all the tears I'd shed before, were not the tears of pride.
They have yet to heal the pain I hide.
Tears, useless tears, every drop a part of me, torn apart,
They never solve a thing, they are but reminders of the pain,
That memory brings.
No I could not let you see, that there were tears, left in me.
I could not share my vulnerability.
To face tomorrow and survive,
The reality of tears is a Truth, I must deny. (smc)

One night as the house settled into silence and my husband slept beside me I slipped quietly out of bed and down the stairs. Silently opening the front door, the rain lashed night rushed to meet me. Only then, completely alone, with rain falling thick and cold and fast, did I allow the pain to take over and the tears to fall. Rain drops mixed with teardrops and disappeared. In the mud of the half- finished subdivision I leaned against a lamp post and collapsed, sliding without thought to the ground. My sobs blended into the darkness of the storm and I wept to the point of exhaustion.

It was that night, alone in the dark that I came to a decision. *(I mentioned I had a peculiar way of looking at my world)* Here goes. I loved my husband, always had and he apparently was not happy. I would let him go! Can you imagine such a thought? I was sure that it would be all right and that those of us who were left would be ok. Insanity right? You bet! I was once again wrong, horribly wrong. I did not fight for him. I believed that he would make the right decision for us, his family. How could he not? I was wrong about that too. He was no longer that strong, if he had ever been.

At this point you are probably thinking that I am out of my mind. You would be wrong. My mind has always been strong. Remember I had come straight from my family home into my young husbands arms. I was innocent, untried and a believer in all things beautiful. I believed in him. At the time I thought that it was right to let him go. I should have held on and fought back, yet looking back with clear vision I wonder now, who was he really or had I never known? The questions were bound to come and I was bombarded by them.

Back then my thoughts went round and round in circles, from loving to rebellion to anger and to hurting, back and forth like a ride that was totally, out of synch, totally out of whack.

I instantly realized that in letting go, I had made a huge mistake. The man that had always thought things through, was gone! The man I had loved, was gone! There was only a stranger that remained, looking like him, sounding like him and wearing his name. Still, somehow, my love remained. I had loved him for so long I didn't know how to do anything else or how to stop the love.

The pain that had come, stayed for a very long time. Much too long.

We needed to talk to our children together and help them understand what was happening and that we both, would always love them. The together thing never happened. I don't remember now, what he said to make me agree to allow him to speak with them alone. I obviously relented. I still trusted!

Right or wrong he wanted to tell them by himself and I went along with that. Another grave mistake made by a woman definitely not thinking straight. He had never been a man that could handle emotion or a scene of any kind and he always needed to make a good impression. The opinion of the world had always been important to him. This is not a judgement, it's just who he was.

He took them to Arbys' restaurant. What was he thinking? Bad idea. You could not get any more public. Perhaps he thought that they would not act up with an audience. Was he out of his mind? I think he must have forgotten that they were only children, his children! Perhaps In his hurry to end his marriage and thinking himself in love, he was excited to share his joy with his kids. Basically, "kids, daddy doesn't love mommy anymore and we are not going to be together. I have found someone else I love and cannot wait for you to meet her."

How sad, how cruel, how utterly selfish and how completely lost, he must have been! The meeting did not go as he had planned. The kids were devastated and they all started to cry. What had he expected?

I cannot begin to imagine what was racing through their young minds but their world had just been tumbled upside down and washed away. I should have been there to help them. I should have stopped him. I should never have let him talk to them alone. I am so very sorry that I allowed this.

Even now I have no clear idea of how he handled the situation that he alone, had created. What exactly had he expected of them? He was the adult here, their father. Where was the love? I know only that this was the defining moment, the trigger, the time, when I finally grew up and stopped believing totally, in this stranger that was no longer my husband. Did I still love him? Probably. Bottom line, on the plus side, I loved my children much more.

A few things of great import happened after that. We had decided on a six week trial to allow him the opportunity to figure things out. He was to go to his parents. I did not realize at the time that his plans were already set in stone, so during that period I tried in various ways to reach him.

On his way out the door he asked me for an additional "$10,000.00" for the business" he said. We had not lost the business at this time. I just looked at him and shook my head saying, "do you realize what it is you are asking of me?' **He said emphatically, "yes I do and it will be all right!"**

I so wanted to believe him. It seemed like a Promise to me at the time. Perhaps there was still a chance for our family. Trusting him one last time, I took that statement to the bank, adding an additional loan against our home. This left the house with disposable assets after expenses, of approximately (nil).

It's funny how old habits like **Trust**, are so difficult to let go of. There are some things the heart just doesn't want to accept and Trust kept getting in my way. In all honesty, after this I never trusted him again. He had made it impossible for me to do so. Bubbles kept bursting, pop, pop, pop. Would they ever stop?

CHAPTER 6

(Things I Did Not Want To Know)

Note: Unbelievably it was just the other day as I was making an attempt to write this book, that a "light dawned." This many years too late. He probably needed that money to set up housekeeping with his girlfriend. I'm glad that hadn't occurred to me way back then. Lucky for him. Talk about innocent. At this distance it no longer matters of course and yet it took a great deal of time before**, "he"** no longer mattered.

This brief flash of light brings another act to the forefront of my mind, another something I did not want to know. It was a few years after he left that I discovered he had also cashed in all the insurance policies for myself and the kids. At that time I was tight for money and a friend suggested that I might be able to borrow on my policy, only surprise, there wasn't one. Shock value, wow! I had just been fired from my terrific job due to being hospitalized. On top of this I had recently purchased a new home in town that would be closing in a couple of months and I was jobless. Suffice it to say, I was just a wee bit stressed.

To add insult to injury one of our closest friends when speaking to my husband on the subject of us, asked point blank, "what about her and the kids, what are you doing about them?" His immediate response was, "she is not getting a dime from me!" I cannot begin to explain how much this statement hurt on top of everything else, when I was finally told**. Why?**

I had stood by him, believed in him, sacrificed for him. We lost two homes prior while he followed his various dreams. What was he talking about? Perhaps who was he talking to is a better question? However, my question will always be, what happened to the husband, I once loved?

(I'm trying to make a point here, people change during major upheavals … Beware, keep safe)

Have you ever thought, **"I don't deserve this!"**
Welcome to my world.

About the things that I did not want to know, the ones that kept on hurting, the actions that were out of character that continued opening wounds, that I was trying to heal, I discovered that my husband no longer existed, not one particle of him remained that could remind me of the man I used to know. Now even my memories were tarnished. He had changed completely. There is no other explanation.

The emotion I felt now was sorrow and loss, for his loss of self. Wrong choices had led him to a place in his mind that even he, must be unaware of. This I must believe. There was one thing I was sure of, he had ceased caring about me, entirely. **<u>Perhaps he had never cared.</u>** For the sake of my children I still needed to reach him.

As I mentioned I write. It is the way I have always communicated, for clarity of self, for the joy of creation, and to reach those that I love. It is the only voice I have. I am communicating now. Are you still listening? There is something here somewhere, which might be important for you to know. I sincerely hope so.

(A thought, an idea, an observation comes and the words drop, one by one upon a blank page. When the words stop the work is done. I believed that I was in control of my writing, but it is not so, for the words carry me to wherever they want me to go. That is how writing works for me. I do not fight it.)

Perhaps you have noticed that I see things differently than most. It is not right or wrong, just me, so as I write this history, I will be adding thoughts that matter to me and the things that I wrote to him. You will see that he doesn't get off scott free, not within the scope of my writing.

I wrote a lot during this whole process, trying to reach him, senseless really! Most of the time I never gave him any of it, so really what did I achieve? Why did I bother? It was a crazy time and I wrote accordingly, from my point of view and sometimes, illogically, from his. Like a roller coaster ride the words ran up hill and down, making little sense at times. Often a little humour went along with a little sad.

One thing about writing it down, it **gets it out.** That's major. Try it! No really. It's a great idea. Nobody said it had to be good, it just needs to come from your heart. It will help to make your Heart, whole once more**. That obviously is the goal!**

Note: If you are hurting right now, going through a mess, out of control, know this, I have learned, <u>**"We hurt in direct proportion to our capacity to love."**</u> **(If you are hurting, you are worth saving.)**

<u>**Secondly: "We are in charge of how much pain and for how long."**</u> Isn't that amazing? Think about it. It's a great theory. Here is how it worked for me.

I took my young son to a therapist hoping he could help him through this transition. When he had seen him he asked me to come into his office. After some discussion he asked me, **"what does the pain look like, describe it, see it. If you can see it, you can handle it."** I realized later that he meant that literally and figuratively. I wondered if the therapist needed a therapist! I tried to do what he said. I replied after some careful thought, **"It's like a huge, square chunk of ice sitting in the middle of my chest. It's heavy and I can't breathe."** His next statement was, **"Visualize. Put your hands on it, lift it out and put in on the corner of my desk for a while, give yourself permission to breathe. When you feel that you need to have the pain back, put it back in but remember, you are the only one who can decide if you have hurt enough."**

This was mind blowing! Once I knew that I had some control over the pain, it made a huge difference. **We hurt but ultimately it is up to us, how severe and for how long. "Visualize!"** It really worked for me. It can work for you too. What do you have to lose? In all honesty it truly helped me dispel some of the pain. I am so very grateful that I took my son to see him and that the therapist wanted to see me too.

CHAPTER 7

My journey continues. I travel each day towards beginnings without end. Endless possibilities surrounded by miracles I **refuse to** see, but they are there.

My eyes allow me to see the beauty all around me, but I am too tied up with Life to be aware of what my eyes have found. I hear voices in my world, the jumble of opinions and emotions and the confusion this can bring and more often than not, I get lost in inconsequential things.

The world is a large and noisy place and in the midst of countless activities and problems and the solving of these, I forget to remember to be, just me.

We have been given the "Gift of Choice." What is it that we are choosing and in so doing, what have we lost, at what cost? If the answer is **Self,** stop, search within and begin again, **for you are on the wrong path!**

Stay true to your own truth for in the end, as youth and beauty fade and memory dims, and strength and courage go wandering, when friends pass beyond the veil and we are all alone, will we be happy with the image that we see?

Stripped of all finery, clearly visible at last and faced with the Truth of Self, are we who we wanted to be or is it a stranger that we see.

Never doubt for one second that we had, no choice, in the end result of who we are. There is always a choice! No matter the journey, the hardship, the pain, we are the sum total of who we chose to become.

What we do, what we think, what we say, will **show** what we have gained. I love who I am, imperfect though that is. At journey's end, will I still have this knowledge?

Life is a remarkable discovery of self, and in the end it is all that we have. Will it be enough? That of course is entirely up to us.

Sorry, I got sidetracked, but know this, your Life is pretty important. Just saying! Think about it. You Matter!

Beginnings Without End

A door closes behind you and locks and you
stand alone at the edge of a great void.
You are confused, cold, scared, without hope.
Sadness and sorrow burrow deep in your
soul as you recall all that is lost.
Do not lose yourself. The Sorrow and Sadness, they will pass.
Let the tears fall, feel each drop, let them
wash the pain from your Heart.
The tracks of your tears are Real, let them work, let them Heal.
When the healing starts, then the Miracles
happen. Allow the Miracles!
Now you are standing at the edge of a great
adventure and new beginnings.
You taste the fear of the unknown and you feel
the excitement of limitless possibilities.
Your eyes feast upon the vast repast of natures'
bounty, its beauty, buds and blooms.
It bursts forth in a myriad of shapes and
colors and scents to entice the pallet.
You partake and are filled with the strength of its goodness.
You have decisions to make, choices. The paths are
everywhere, their destinations, anywhere.
The only possible stumbling block is you.
You step forward with Courage,
And Faith catches you in her arms, and Hope takes
you by the hand, leading you into sunlight.
It is the sun that guides your steps by day, and
a night you sleep beneath the stars.
Daily you learn and you grow and you take from
the past only memories to treasure,
But you never look back. The Chains that bound
you in Pain, lay behind you, forgotten,
Like the broken baubles of a child at play.
You are no longer, that child.

Actions equal reactions and you realize that
you must be responsible for yours,
And that you have no control over the actions of another.
This knowledge sets you free. Your steps
quicken and you find you are running,
Not away from your Life, but rather towards
it. You race the wind and you win,
And it's at your back and it's pushing you forward.
Laughter fills the air, and a forgotten something
surrounds you. It's called Joy.
You realize that you are happy! Your great adventure
led you to Self. You are no longer lost.
Live the Gift of Life you were given. Thank God for
the Miracle of you and always remember,
Endings are only Beginnings, Beginnings Without End……. (smc)

CHAPTER 8

I am pretty sure this book should be taking a more direct course of action and yet I know without all my side trips, the picture could never be clear. If you have gotten this far with me, you may believe and rightly so, that I was lost and wandering, yet that is no longer true. Despite your doubts I ask you most humbly to stick it out. There has to be some insane reason that I feel I must follow the dictates of my mind and unload the priceless gems that I have discovered on Life's journey to the here and now. I do know that if I don't put my thoughts to paper as it's happening those thoughts are lost forever into the great unknown. There are a million ways to capture in words, what you want to say, a million words configured differently that reproduce our thoughts.

I am constantly learning, sometimes ever so slowly it seems, but I now know that for every road I travel, there is a reason for that journey. For every life I touch or that touches mine, I must be grateful, for there is wisdom and knowledge to be gained. Whether it be through joy or pain, we learn, we grow strong, we start to remember in the deepest, sweetest part of us, who we really are. I am no longer afraid, for I am no longer lost. I marvel at my age, well over half a century and yet I don't feel old. I may move a little slower, forget a little more, see less clearly the physical world and yet I know I have gained a little wisdom, grown a little stronger, become more tolerant. I have even sometimes known myself to show patience. My courage has never failed me and my Faith amazingly, holds firm. Against all odds, I beat the odds …. How odd!

Now I take nothing for granted. If life has taught me anything, it has taught me that. There are no guarantees. We have but today, this hour, this minute, this second, to be happy. With only the Faith that has always sustained me, I embrace this moment and the Gift of Life I have been given. It is enough!

What about you my friend? Who are you really? Do you want to know? What makes you happy? Can you remember when you were? Is your life a nightmare of struggle and pain or a mountain of miracles only you can name? Do you have the Courage to ask yourself the hard questions and the strength to listen for the answers that are surely there? Remember there is only one person you are accountable to, that person is you. Take the time to learn your own truth. We do not always ask for the hands we are dealt, but always the choices to play that hand are ours alone. By the way, "Life is not always fair," so expect it not to be. The people you love, will let you down. It's called being human. You will feel pain, it means you have a heart. These things are good. Take Heart.

My how my thoughts have wandered. I get to rambling. Could it be age?

Back on track. I wrote crazy off the wall things, to my husband, for my husband, from my perspective and from his, if you can imagine that. I tried to see his life at this time from his point of view. I tried to understand. I still loved him. I thought we had 6 weeks to work this out. So here goes.

It's personal but I think I need to share. You probably need to know, that in the midst of the storm, anything goes. (Except violence). There are always parts of ourselves that we keep hidden, for safety's sake. The face we show the world is often not the heart, that needs to be heard. These are some of my writings as I tried to reach my one time husband, my one time friend.

There were always unannounced flashes of pain.

I went through periods of appeal, memories shared, anger, humility, sarcasm and the ridiculous. It is this last one that I will impart to you now. My husband was apparently searching for my replacement and I stubbornly wanted to apply for the job. Hence the (Ridiculous bordering on tragic.)

I think I must have personally covered almost every emotion known to woman or man when trying to reach, my man.

<u>#1 This bit of writing is titled **"The Resume"** Dated: August 26, 1987</u>
<u>(Time frame: 1 month and 4 days from the</u>
<u>date I was made aware of his needs)</u>

<u>Job Description:</u> That of **Wife** to local publisher, or ad manager or other line of work.

<u>Personal History:</u> Age 38 years young and improving daily.

<u>Health</u>: excellent for my age

<u>Address:</u> wherever you are   **<u>S. I. N. #</u>** (sins relatively few)

<u>Married:</u> 18 years currently   **<u>Children:</u>** 3 beauties. (They remind me of you)

<u>Weight:</u> 109 lbs and counting down until you come to your senses.

<u>Qualification:</u>

I love my husband, great rapport with prospective employer, three children you love.

Would expect no pay or remuneration, hard worker, excel at any challenge.

Two jobs at once is not uncommon. Honest, Trustworthy, Faithful, of strong Faith.

Humility is a strength when combined with love. A natural intelligence.

School of the Heart: Courses, 1. Understanding, 2. Love, 3. Compassion

<u>Note:</u> I am of a forgiving nature, (better than I knew) it's automatic

Please feel free to call at any time to arrange an interview. I will not disappoint you! I feel that I have the qualifications that you are seeking in a wife, helpmate and mother. I always bring with me a positive attitude and a sincere desire to achieve, no matter what the odds. The qualities that I possess are of priceless value and are of long standing. (Until forever) My values do not change, only improve.

I feel sure that you could grow accustomed to my face, my voice, my dynamic personality. I am a little emotional but I am real. That should account for something to a discerning man. I promise you years of faithful service and a life full of love, happiness, laughter. I will bring you joy! You have but to remember. "Ask and It shall be given unto you, seek and you shall find." (Scripture)

The above for your consideration: I remain, Faithfully Yours ….

Your wife …… **(Note: Resume never sent!)**

(Written prior to our separation for our 16th
wedding anniversary 1970-1986)
<u>**Poem # 2: Then and Now**</u>

Then I gave to you of my youth, my innocence and my trust.
You gave to me of yourself, and that was good.
For you I have a great respect, a confident
dependence in your judgement.
I have an unshakeable belief in you, who you are, what you are.
To be worthy of you, my husband and our
children, is what I ask of myself,
It's what I strive to achieve. I pray to be always
what you need and want of me.
I loved you then a little. I love you today with a love that will not die.
Tomorrow, I will love you more. Smc

(I was young and foolish and apparently, knew him not. Go figure)

(He left September 2, 1987)
Poem # 3 : Despair

Despair, when you feel it, it's everywhere.
It hangs heavy, tugging at your heart.
It clamps like a vise about your throat.
It attacks your whole body. It causes physical pain.
I pray I never feel it again.
Heart, body and soul, all need repair.
The sun mocks and laughter makes you cry.
Hope deserts you and life just passes you by.
Sometimes you feel, you just want to die.
Life just isn't fair.
I would grasp at happiness, but it's just not there.
Hope is all but gone, Faith still lingers on.
How could something so right, turn out so very wrong?
Despair…. Why do I still care? Smc

(Written September 25/87)
Poem # 4 : Answer Despair

A new day will come tomorrow and again tomorrow,
Waiting just for you.
The sun will rise tomorrow and the sky will still be blue.
And survival is for the fittest and it's all up to you.
The strength, it is within you.
Family, friends and God, will see you through. Smc

(Written Sept 10, 1987)
Thoughts #5 : Dearest Husband

I realize that you are after all, very human, subject to all the frailties, misconceptions and rationalizations practiced by the people as a whole. You have somehow lost sight of truth and right. You have replaced love and caring, with self. It is all so very sad.

I will always love the man you once were. Someone else can love the man you have become. There is no comparison, so there really is justice if we but seek and find it. I no longer have to feel so much pain, for someone who no longer exists. The pain that is left is still too great.

What you are doing will never be right. Perhaps for others, but never for you. You spoke to me of foundations and that ours was strong. We would have made it, beautifully. We always have. I know it, you know it and God knows it. For whatever reasons, you walked away. I realize now, you are a coward. How sad.

Nothing you can tell yourself will justify these actions. You must live with it. You are basing a few months against a lifetime, a wife and a family. We had the world on a string and you let it go.

How firm is your foundation? You are trying to build a life on a foundation based on the ashes and destruction of human suffering. The seeds you have planted will not grow, unless nurtured from the evil that begat them. As you sow also shall you reap. It is therefore a life wasted, many lives, because evil in the end, will not survive.

Good, Truth and Right are the basis for life. You have forgotten. Only you can make it right. (smc)

Excerpts from letters written to him

"In sickness and in health, for better or worse, for richer or for poorer." You were only there for the good times I guess, my big strong husband. The man I looked up to with pride. When I needed you for a change, you were not at my side.

I am sorry I am in your way, but you see honey, giving to you and loving you, comes as natural to me as night follows day. You have taken the easy road. Most people do. Remember there is a road home, if you can but find it. How long the door will be open to you, I do not know. Happiness depends on it. We are four hearts beating just for you. That is our truth.

Written June 14, 1988
(10 months after the storm had hit …still communicating)
Poem #6 : Remember When

Remember when our bodies were young, healthy and strong,
When our lives were before us and nothing could go wrong.
When our goals were reachable and we ourselves were teachable.
Remember when love was brand new, when
everything we did, was fun to do.
When laughter came easily and tears were few.
Do you remember?
Remember when qualities like, patience and understanding,
Listening and caring, giving and sharing were all around us.
Do you remember?
Remember when Trust was something we took for granted,
When life together, was all that mattered.
Do you remember … Do you remember when?
My one time Husband, my one time Friend. (smc)

**Poem # 7 … Written March 30, 1988 … (I wrote
his obituary … for me he had died)
Note: (this poem was never given)
I know this is off the deep end! You will find
you do what is needed to survive.
Who does this? (Me) Perhaps you will understand the need.**

(C.E.M)

In remembrance of my Husband.
In my Heart and Mind, I buried my Husband
The end of January 1988.
It seems he had been suffering from a fatal disease
And he was too weak to fight it.
He contracted it in the summer of 1987,
And did not survive!
It was life that caused his death.
Not Life itself …. But how he lived it.
When I remember, I will remember only,
That which was good ….in the Husband that I loved.
Otherwise …. I shall remember …. Nothing at all.
This is my choice … I so choose!
Smc

Hello again, I'm back. Are you still hanging in there? As I stated earlier, there is no set course for this journey that we didn't want to take. You may feel at this point that I am letting you down. You would be wrong. I'm with you all the way. I want you Strong!

From this distance I cannot even remember if I gave him anything that I wrote. I wonder if it would have made a difference, yet it no longer matters. As you can see he didn't get off easily. I was nothing if not relentless. A little rebellion was going on just to hold onto my sanity. I was still trying to reach the husband that I loved, even then. He was nowhere to be found. Just for future reference, loving is never wrong.

Remember, **"Let your love so shine that the darkness no longer holds fear."** If you have done all you can, you can walk away, conscience clear, free to love once more. That is your Right!

CHAPTER 9

The date is January 3 and the clock has ticked us all into a brand new year. 2015 is here. What, I wonder, are we going to do with it? I for one am happy to still be here. I have always known that family is everything and that love is what makes it work. Talking about love!

My father passed on to the next page of his travels in October of last year. He was ready to go. The siblings and the grandchildren miss him terribly, but he left us a tremendous Legacy. This poem was written and inserted into a scrapbook of a life well lived for our dads' 80th birthday celebration. Of course as in all things I never finished his huge book till thanksgiving of 2012. I was only three years late with it. This poem is titled.... **"OUR FATHER"**

"OUR FATHER"

Thank you for the journey that is your life.
For the Faith in God, that you always followed.
For the Beauty of you Heart, which you continue to use.
For your individuality, not bowing to peer pressure.
For the Strength of you Convictions, and following through.
For Courage in the face of Adversity,
And Perseverance, when the road was less travelled.
For your Creativity, Your Genius, Your Stubbornness,
Frustrating as that sometimes is.
For the Sheer Joy with which you embrace your Life.
You have always walked tall and proud,
Yet with a Sweet Humility, few would understand.
You are your own man, always were, always will be.
There were the hard times, the lean times, the good times,
But at all times we were wrapped safe, in the Arms of Love.
There is no greater Gift than this. We are truly Blessed.
Thank you for the Legacy …. " Of a Life Well Lived."
May we pass this on to our children …and they, to theirs …. (smc)

I woke this morning at 3:33 am. I could not go back to sleep. At 4:44 am I quietly slipped out of bed and wandered down the hall. I have learned that it is useless to recapture sleep. For over an hour my mind has been meandering through my life, sending me down memory lane in no organized manner what so ever as my thoughts drifted to roads travelled and those I have not taken.

I was thinking about this book that has currently taken up centre stage on a day to day basis. Beyond all the things I should be doing, is the wish that I could unravel, with mere words, the rest of my story.

As memory fades, the facts from this great distance are decidedly blurred, and yet my outlook now has a clarity I could not uncover in the midst of my storm. I have taken to asking my daughter time frames. She was 14 and just starting high school when tragedy struck. It is never a good time to lose a dad and my children suffered greatly.

The repercussions are resounding to this day. They were 14, 11, and 8, all old enough to feel confusion and pain and loss, although they never understood the why and neither did I.

I state again, categorically, that I would not have wanted to miss this nightmare journey that I did not want to make, for unravelling life's mysteries has brought tremendous gains.

However, with all my heart, I wish that my children had been spared the sacrifices, the pain and the insecurities that resulted. I still can see the effects of those events through the life choices of my children.

Doubts, trust, and fear undermined their personal journey at various stages of their lives as they travelled towards sunshine and light. Through all of this, they grew to be strong, intelligent adults, blessed with Hearts that work and they are not afraid to use those hearts.

They are all amazing parents. Their children will all be raised, surrounded by Love, Security and Truth. I now have no fear for their futures.

It has taken us all, many years to come to a greater understanding of the **"Human Condition."**

CHAPTER 10

Back Then: Like a battlefield, that is what my life became as bridges were burned, cutting off communications and fires raged and needed to be put out in all directions and fighting for territorial rights, which couch and how many beds, and are you going to sell the house? Questions, questions, questions! So many questions to be answered as the storm continued and confusion fought for supremacy.

Taking a deep breath and bringing logic into the equation my answers were, there are four of us and so we needed beds and couches and tables and chairs and fridge and stove for my family. With his desertion they had become my children and my responsibility and rightly so. I was the only one left to protect them and so I would do the very best I could.

He would receive what we were able to give him and I had no intention of supporting his new family. He was currently setting up housekeeping and she was bringing her four children into the equation. In reality he now had two families and seven children. Looking back I guess when he asked for an additional $10,000.00 for the business on his way out the door, he meant his monkey business. That means, unfortunately, that I did in reality, support them. How sad.

Instead of the six week trial period for him to find himself he forgot to inform me that he had already made his decision and was making provisions immediately for his new family. His words, "**Yes I know what I am asking and it will be all right**." as he walked out the door, I foolishly, believing him to be the man I loved, trusted him **one last time,** then I trusted no more.

The result was more equity gone and a higher mortgage on the matrimonial home. That is what I received as he waltzed away to start a new life without feeling or thought of the damage these actions were doing to the ones left behind.

Visitation: Practically Nil

Ours was not the typical agreement where the one gone would have visitation with his children on say, Tuesday and Wednesday and every other weekend. It could easily have been that and more once I got used to the fact that I was now totally alone.

Ours worked out to be hit or miss, usually missed, where he forgot to call them or he picked them up only for a short hop to the nearest donut shop for approximately ½ an hour. The children wilted under the neglect.

My eldest, my daughter who had always been the apple of her fathers' eye, was crushed with the knowledge that her dad was now taking his new daughter to the Library and helping her with her homework. It did not matter that my daughter did not need this help. She spoke to me about this. Looking back I realized she had been correct. He had not spent a lot of time with his own children. He always seemed too busy with his own pursuits.

Due to the fact that he hardly ever came for them it became necessary for me to get involved and in touch with him. To spare their feelings I would use the phone in my bedroom and make the call without their knowledge.

"Hi, the kids miss you so much. They need to see you. Could you please come and get them or at least give them a call?" Those calls were hard for me, not knowing who would pick up the phone and it was so close to our separation. Just hearing his voice could make me cry.

Sometimes the call would have a positive effect and he would call them or come to get them, but more often than not he did not show. I have absolutely no idea why. Regardless, the children suffered. It's hard to figure out how a man that was so well loved could disappear so completely. Who was he, really, this stranger who was acting so very strange. I began to believe that he was someone that I didn't want to know.

I will always remember standing on the steps of our home as my children climbed into his car for the very first time and I stood there crying as they disappeared around the corner, feeling lost without them. That is when the nightmare, the reality of it, hit me right between the eyes. He had taken my children. I was fast learning all the lessons I never thought I would have to learn. I had to scramble to stay on my feet and walk one step ahead of the next catastrophe, the next decision, the next blast of pain. It didn't make me weak, it didn't make me wrong. It left me a mother and that made me strong. I was pretty much on my own and I carried a heavy load, lightly and with love.

"Alone"

Alone and lonely, it's frightening
All by myself in a world full of people.
I feel the cold, I hear the silence,
I know the emptiness.
There is no direction, no purpose, no meaning,
And I am not special,
In this world full of people.
Time is like a drop of rain,
That falls and then disappears,
Mixed with the salt of my tears.
Alone and lonely, it's frightening,
All by myself in a world full of people. (smc)

CHAPTER 11

"To thine own self be true," six simple words that equal all Truth. **"Remember in the deepest, sweetest part of you, where no one else can see, patiently waits the person you were always meant to be."**

The Lord made each of us perfect in our own unique way, not so we would not make mistakes but so that we would know, what mistakes we were making, and then He gave to us the tools to overcome them. To some He gave pieces of His Heart, so beautiful. To others He gave something called intelligence. Wisdom, He imparted to a few choice spirits and to all of us, He gave Eternal Truth. He gave us Strength to use whenever we had need of it, for as long as we each shall live and added unfailing Courage to face danger, (real or imagined). His final Gift was a Soul, which would always bring us back to Him, when we were ready. He surrounded us with Miracles!

Somewhere, within the space of a heartbeat, awaits your Miracle. You are that Miracle. No longer deny your **God given right to Happiness!** Do not allow the memories that immobilize you, to shadow your days upon this earth. With justified anger send those demons away. They have only the Power you gave them. Seize today and keep it for yourself. Never forget, "Self Matters."

So whenever you think you are lost, know you are not. Whenever your strength fails, know you have merely forgotten it is there. When you are hurting and in despair, turn to your Heart, God is there. Do not look in the mirror in search of self, for all truth lies within the Heart and Soul. Therein lies your beauty.

When you believe in the Miracle of you, **you will reflect this Truth**! To deny self is to die a little each day. Life is a Gift worth living. For one moment in time, take the time to listen to your hearts deepest desires, then follow through.

You are a Gift, God gave to the world. Embrace it. <u>"To thine own self … be true!"</u>

<u>Random Thoughts</u>

As time passed and life continued, I moved with it. The pain lessened and the days worked themselves into a manageable pattern. I started to breathe again. I began to feel that I would survive this.

There were flashes of pain out of nowhere which struck like lightning to disturb an otherwise ordinary day. Those moments were rare, bearable, short lived. They existed only as long as I allowed them any power.

I'd be driving along on my way to work on a summer day, minding my own business, at peace and a song would come on the radio and drag me forcefully back in time, just for a minute. For that moment I would be swamped, defenseless, engulfed in remembered pain and then I would let it go. It was a concerted effort of will.

(I was still young enough to bounce back way back then. Today I don't bounce as well and if I do, I could physically hurt something. Just stating the facts.)

These episodes seemed to happen when I was alone and not interacting with others. Often while driving my car on my way to somewhere and for absolutely no feasible reason, I would find myself crashing, (not my car) but rather swamped with memories, not all of them beautiful. For times like these I developed a **mantra.** Amazingly it helped.

Immediately, gripping the steering wheel tightly with both hands, I'd say with passion, **"pull up, pull up, you are diving out of control and you are going to crash!"** Figuratively, I would pull up on that steering wheel as if I were piloting a plane and bring the nose up out of a dive to land safely back on solid ground. It never failed to bring me back, but fast.

It's funny how little crutches can keep us from a potential fall.

The mantra was great and nobody knew what was happening for I was internalizing within the confines of my mind. I could use it in any given situation where I found myself floundering, out of my depth. This safety net was a perfect foil for any hazards I encountered in the day to day.

My first major nose dive occurred when my little girl and I attended church up in Toronto. It was a special occasion and we were going into a church full of strangers for the Christening of my baby niece. The day was perfect until the congregation began to sing, **"When there's love at home, love at home. Peace and beauty here abide when there's love at home."**

I lost it, totally. I got all chocked up and started to cry uncontrollably. <u>**There was no love at home.**</u> Love had died! Once started, the tears kept coming like a ship cleaving through the storm tossed waves with water crashing on the slippery deck. I never carried tissue. I was broken and I held nothing back.

I stood up and stumbled out of the church pulling my little girl along with me.

I was a total wreck and so very ashamed of being weak and causing such an awful scene. I could no longer trust that I would not break down in public and so for a very long time I stopped going to Church.

In church everyone sat in families and my family was broken. It was too sad. Until this moment most of my breakdowns were conducted in private. **This one scared me.** I thought that I was doing great and then I was not. I was understandably, **<u>Swamped, and still Lost!</u>**

CHAPTER 12

Incredibly, self- discovery happens when we least expect it. I was learning so much. It was at this time that I discovered I was a wee bit stubborn! Where did this stubbornness come from or had it always been there, but not necessary? It seemed to me that I was only stubborn about things that were important, things that mattered to me or when I was right. Perhaps I had decided to make a stand and take control of something.

On a lighter note, looking back to before the storm, I realize that somewhere in my makeup there had always been a defining moment or two where I would enjoy testing the waters, plunging my oar into the river and diverting the natural flow of life, just a little. A ripple here a wave there.

For Example:

I love clothes, I think they are fun. I put them together in my own particular fashion and strut. The secret to clothes is **"attitude,"** take a stride with pride. Be a little ahead of your time.

When I was young I was kind of cute and could pull off just about anything. I love the unusual, the unique and just to put a jarring note to a perfect ensemble I would undoubtedly add a weird pair of shoes. "Did you notice me yet?"

Currently, the weird shoes have a practical purpose, they are called orthotics. I get all dressed up to go dancing and add my running shoes with every outfit. Good thing that I started being unorthodox at a young age, making a statement.

The shoes elicit many comments and all from women whose feet are hurting in their stylish heels. Who knows, perhaps I will start a new trend and be a leader for the senior sector. I already have one courageous convert.

For Example: When I worked at the Public Utilities as head cashier it was my job to tally up the cash and cheques, roll the coins, (we did that way back then) get the deposit ready for the bank and stuff it all into an actual bank bag. It looked like a bank bag! Then I would take myself, dressed in my high heels, (work standards) and smashing outfit outside and down the sidewalk two blocks to the bank on the corner.

Looking back on this I wonder why I was not accosted. Anyone could have literally grabbed that bag and run off and I would never have caught them. Especially not in heels.

Into the bank I would go for the daily shuffle, shuffle, scuffle, taking mincing baby steps up to the teller. In those days prior to bank machines, if you were doing banking you were standing in an unending line of impatient customers.

Bored out of my mind and not enjoying the shuffle, I wondered what exactly would happen if I refused to move the next ½ foot. The shuffle started as the next customer made it safely to the teller. All those in line ahead of me jumped in to fill the void. It was a coordinated move. I stood my ground. This floor space was mine! I refused to move. I waited.

Those behind me were confused. Their imaginary weight pushed heavily upon my back. I could feel them breathing. I was smiling and wondering what they were thinking. Really, where exactly did they think they were going?

They settled back down, but I did not back down and for the fun of it, as the line moved one more time, again I did not move forward. I was still smiling as the line behind me leaned in to move.

I was no longer bored. If this had happened today I know someone behind me would have shouted … "Move your butt, lady." It would not have been road rage but line rage.

I guess you could safely say it wasn't stubbornness so much as pushing the borders. I would quietly, without harmful intent, push the borders of society's acceptance or tolerance for the hell of it, for the fun of it. Inquiring minds want to know ... (what If?)

And so the border pushing, free spirited, shy young lady that could accomplish anything, did!

When faced with the irrevocable, without a plan, without a safety net, at one point hospitalized and faced unfairly with unemployment, she proved unstoppable.

Sheer determination and courage kept her motoring along, side stepping obstacles, pushing into the unknown, running, until once again she ran free of the disasters that had tried to trash her life and the lives of her children.

It was not allowed! It would never be allowed!

Now I am ahead of myself, but I wanted you to know we made it through the storm ... Intact.

CHAPTER 13

Selling our home:

Getting down to basics, of course I had to sell our home that next spring. To continue on with the tremendous debt load now attached to it was financial suicide. My job was great but it was after all, commission based. I admit I was scared. I buckled under the pressure and put our home on the market. My husband of course was relieved. Home # 3 gone. My real estate pals were well aware that mine was a marriage breakup and I was too stressed, too scared and too worried about my children to put up much of a fight. It sold quickly for much less than market value. Someone got a great deal.

Note: Unfortunately, its human nature to take advantage of those who hit rock bottom and so there was nothing left to show for all the years of hard work and sacrifice. Everything was gone.

The sale displaced my children once again. Nothing was certain, nothing was familiar. Circumstances were tossing them in too many directions and taking them away from their friends, which was crucial. Life would never be the same again and I could do nothing to stop the insanity. Our world became a huge question mark. For my children, moving meant leaving their support system, their friends. I was determined to get them back in the area as soon as humanly possible.

My family and I landed in a heap on my parents' doorstep and thankfully without hesitation they took us in and slowly loved us back to sanity. I can never repay them for the sacrifices they made or all the love they gave. I will be eternally grateful. They saved my life, such as it was at the time and my children will always remember the love. Someone took a picture of us at that time, standing under the giant shade tree in grandma's front yard. I was shattered when I saw that picture and I never let them see it. It was one of the saddest most pathetic pictures I can ever recall seeing. I barely recognized that it was us. Pitiful. I ripped it into tiny pieces and threw it in the garbage where it belonged. I vowed then that we would come about. I do not know how to sail a boat but I was determined to fly. In the face of any and all challenges we would survive and thrive.

I had always believed that love was everything. On a wing and a Prayer, I hoped that it would be enough for my babies. Days, weeks, months passed and I was able to buy them a new home. It was an old town home backing onto the train tracks, so close that the train, as it rumbled through, shook the foundations and rattled the chandelier, but it was home, ours and we loved it. We were in their school district, with their friends. So far I had been able to keep them in the zone with as little change geographically, as possible. They needed nothing more to think about, especially not me. Remember the girl with the "wooden smile." Somehow I had to keep smiling.

The kids must never, for any reason, have to worry about me. I could do this. I was the adult. I was the Parent. I was their mom, and they were, **"My greatest Treasure**."

I fixed up that little townhouse and made it a home. It was adorable and I realized I had a flair, a creative touch that I had been unaware of. I sold that home for more than any other in the complex. It was quite an achievement at the time.

I put an offer on a brand new raised bungalow in a quiet court just up the street. We were on our way. The children and I were excited, but wait I'm getting ahead of myself here. All things are not guaranteed, (tell me about it) and my wonderful job selling new homes came into jeopardy. Actually much worse than that. Tragically, without warning or cause, it came to an end. **The boss fired me.** It's a whole other story and one more fence I had to climb. This new explosion of all our plans, rocked my world. Bursting bubbles exploding, pop, pop pop. Concentrate on the immediate, hold on, breathe, over and over again this is what I repeated.

The boss fired me!　　　How dare she!　　　The Bitch!

I was angry. Needless to say I had the right to be angry, but I did not have the time to follow through with you know who, "the boss." Let me explain. I loved my job. I worked for a great builder. The new homes were in my zone area. My Partner was beautiful, intelligent, professional, a real lady and she taught me well. We were friends. Our boss was something else.

I was excited about my move in a month to our brand new raised bungalow with attached garage, and dealing well with the ramifications of the break up or so I thought. The problem seems to be that I did not have time to deal with that particular problem, the break up. I was too busy staying one step ahead of any and all disasters. I should have taken the time to deal with my state of heart and my state of mind.

Lets' get back to the boss. There is something insanely insecure about some of the women with **"Power"** in the work force. I state emphatically, only some of the women. (I personally think most women are great). The others have an intense need to Control! Freakishly so. They need to be needed. If this need is not met they need to Destroy. Unfortunately, I have encountered this many times. Such was the temperament of this woman. ***Note:*** *I did not need her and I never kiss ass.* I was great at my job. Suffice it to say, she fired me. **Her excuse:** I was in the hospital and unable to do my job. How sweet was that? At the lowest most vulnerable time of my life, without cause or compassion she took away my livelihood and left me and my children destitute. If I hadn't been so busy fighting my way back to normal, I would have taken her to court for wrongful dismissal.

There is no doubt that I would have won that case. None what so ever. Young single mom with three children to provide for, an excellent job performance record and just coming out of the hospital under doctors care. As it was, what can I say? With the loss of my job, I was but mere inches away from plunging back into the darkness that I was slowly but steadily leaving behind.

CHAPTER 14

Please hang in there and let me explain how all this came about. Once again I was scrambling to escape the waves washing over me, with no life preserver in sight. For clarification, I owned a new home, the mortgage was already in place, the kids were packed and we were moving in a month, and I had … No job!

Panic city. Wow! This slightly huge problem was definitely not going away. I, who had never been without a job, and usually a good one, was unemployed, but hopefully not unemployable.

Have you ever been so riveted on what had to be done and doing it, that you totally forgot to look in the mirror and see that you, yourself, were heading for trouble. So there you have it. I forgot to look after me. A simple matter really, but I didn't do it. I believed I was ok.

Sometimes when that happens you have what is known as a, **"breakdown."** Those come in various shapes and sizes and to each one of us it will be unique. With all I had been doing to stay afloat, I had not taken the time to deal with the destruction of my marriage. Add to this that there had been no time.

For the record, the ending of a marriage is very high on the list of major life catastrophes. There are stages of Grief that must be gone through as **"rite of passage."** Things like fear, loss, anger, loneliness, rejection, trust, insecurities, betrayal, hit after hit after hit. Boom, Boom, Boom. Bubbles Bursting like a world exploding.

<u>New Job</u>

It was the long thanksgiving weekend. My partner had booked off the time for a family holiday at her cottage. I would be manning the new home site alone that weekend. No problem. The weather was perfect and believe it or not I had learned that holidays are the best selling days at new home sites. I was pumped. I love to be busy. I had a great product and location, location, location.

My first day was crazy busy with tons of positive energy from prospective purchasers. I was tired but happy. I walked around at the end of the day locking doors and closing down the site. As I pulled out the desk drawer for my purse my back went into spasm. I could not move. Pain ripped through my body. **"Not now, please!"** I silently prayed. I could not walk, could hardly move, I definitely could not drive my car home, although the distance was short. I had to call my father who came by and pretty much picked me up and drove me home. The townhouse was two stories and there was no way I was going to make it up those stairs. I spent the night on the couch.

Too much weight can sink a perfectly healthy ship and I was the mother ship carrying the mother lode. Stresses I was unaware of or those that I had pushed aside to deal with later, were creating a minor but hopefully reparable break in the very structure of my life. These feelings, these emotions, this pain, that I had pushed aside so I could ride out the storm, would no longer wait quietly in the background. I would have to deal with it.

I was under attack and too busy plugging the holes of each new situation to pay attention. I was going down for the third time. I had to be stopped.

Just so you know, we are walking miracles and if we don't pay attention, our bodies will jump into rescue mode and get us the help we need one way or the other. My mind did not break, it never breaks, unlike my heart which is fragile, and so my body broke down instead, under the strain. It just ceased to move.

In self- preservation, stress searched for and found the weakest part of me so that I would pay attention to what it was I needed. I needed to look after me, but before I did that I had one more thing to do, and the time was now.

My mind jumped into overload. There was a major problem to be solved. I had a job to do and do it I would, somehow. Lying on the couch I lifted the phone beside me and quickly dialed my best friend. I told her what had happened and asked if she would be available to go into the office with me the next day and walk the clients through the model homes. This was my responsibility.

I would be available, chained to the desk, to answer any questions or type up offers that needed to be done. Remember it was thanksgiving weekend and that is family time. She came like the trooper she is and together we got the job done. As I said, "my friends got me through."

Bottom line, that night I ended up in the hospital, in traction and screaming with pain. After having previously delivered 3 large healthy babies and not making a sound, you can gage how much pain existed at this time. It was tremendous.

The nurses gave me a needle and magically the pain disappeared. It was wonderful. I can't remember what drug it was but for it to work immediately it must have been addictive and I do not like pills. I soon asked them to take me off it.

I had never been in traction before and was trussed up with weights and pulleys, but it was working, putting space between the discs of my back. I do not remember how long this lasted. A surgeon came in to talk to me about getting fitted for a back brace that would be specially made to lift and hold in place a back that was not cooperating. It was similar to the old fashioned corsets with whale bone stays and I would be required to wear it constantly for approximately six week. I promised him I would do this.

A psychologist was called in who was a little concerned about depression and confused as to why I would take myself off all medications. Apparently few do that. He was also totally aware of my current situation from start to finish, gratis my family doctor who had asked him to consult. I thanked him for coming and told him I was good, and that I just needed to get home. I had matters I needed to deal with immediately. I needed to be with my children. I was once again walking, that is what mattered and it was great and I was very grateful. I guess you may be wondering why the saga with my back. Simple enough. The crux of the matter was my boss deemed me unfit for work and not available to do the job and she fired me. It was just that simple for her.

I had only been out of commission for perhaps two weeks and my partner had covered for me and yet there was no stopping the boss.

There I stood, single mom, 3 kids, no job! No job, no money! Well I didn't have time to take her to court as she deserved but they say all things come to those that wait and I believe that a short time later, she was no longer in the business. Enough said.

By the way I just remembered her name but it's not important. She is not important.

"I state here and now, you must let go of all things toxic."

As I said I was unemployed, but not unemployable, thank goodness. As a last resort I took my pride and tossed it aside and acknowledged that sometimes we all need help.

I walked into social services and told them part of my story. I was scared, humbled and needy and there was no place else to turn. I needed to look after my children. My ex-husband was in no position to help us at this time.

I was panicked and had absolutely no idea what to expect from this office.

There I was met by a lovely young woman. (I was 38 at the time and feeling old). After our interview and my application I showed her my Resume. She looked it over and then went to the window and stared down at the street. I thought she was thinking something over. As it turned out, she was.

"We just had a job opening with social services and the deadline was today. I think that you would qualify. I am going to call over and see if I can get you an interview".

Holy cow, she was amazing and I was so fortunate. Talk about timing. Someone was looking after me. The very next day I went for the interview and two weeks later I was offered the job.

It was a Miracle, my Miracle. I was overjoyed. I had a job and they would top up my salary till I got back on my feet. Now I was humbled and grateful.

"Simply Said"

Humility … that is what life has taught me,
And a special kind of pride, few would
understand. I believe in who I am.
I take the good out of the bad and turn it around.
It works beautifully, I have found.
Giving beyond society's accepted measure, and
building friendships, that last forever.
Strength is something I have always known, it allows
me to stand without fear …. on my own.
Faith … In Gods' Holy Plan, Helps me to
remember always … who I am.
Forgiveness comes naturally to me … for I have always believed,
That goodness exists … beyond what our eyes
can see. Hate will never be my Reality.
I believe in the Power of Love … It works for me.
Beyond all the pain I have ever known, Rises in
beauty …. All the love I have been shown.
Beyond all the Riches …. I do not own, Are
Memories to treasure … that are mine alone.
Beyond all the Trials … that I must face, Lies a
Powerful, Wonderful, Healing … Faith!
I have all that I will ever need … Simply said ….
I have been blessed indeed. (smc)

There was however, one condition that I had known nothing about. Apparently a parent is responsible for their children financially and as my husband was unable to pay support or very little at this time, I was informed that I would have to place him with Support and Custody. This was mandatory, no excuses allowed.

Where flowers bloom, weeds abound. This was a major problem for me.

Let me explain my convoluted thinking. If you remember I was still in love with my errant husband or so I believed. I know, what can I say? More bubbles needed bursting until I faced my reality. Bring them on. Pop, pop, pop. Let those bubbles never stop.

Seriously, what kind of a fool was I? It also became evident that my ex was not enthralled with the idea of support and custody, not at all. He was really quite vocal about this, but that is for later or perhaps not at all. Really, it's better left alone.

Support and Custody:

That is what it was called way back then. I didn't want to do it, not to him.

You would think that after all he had put us through, this would be easy for me and yet I dragged my feet every step of the way. Standing in that line waiting to speak to a counsellor was like waiting to meet my executioner.

How do you explain **"wrong,"** for that is what it felt like? I felt guilty, sordid, dirty, mean and yet really there was no alternative. Up until now I had been handling my finances wonderfully. It had not mattered about support, for my job had been, pretty terrific.

Now, if I did not submit a claim for support for my children from their father, then I would receive no assistance. I was in dire need of help and health benefits. My hands were tied.

All that I had held dear, all that I had always believed, was dissipating, bubbles bursting one by one, by one. Pop, pop, pop …. Bursting Bubbles Dropped.

Note:

Unbeknownst to me, repercussion for these actions that were forced upon me, were to be in my future and I was not prepared for the fallout.

When the time came I was blown away, like ashes from the flames.

On second thought I will not impart the rest of this particular episode. Suffice it to say, this is not something I ever want to remember. It was my own personal nightmare. (End of this story.)

CHAPTER 15

A new day dawned, and I started my new job. It was exciting, interesting, enlightening. I was in a position of helping others and everything was brand new. I jumped in with both feet and never looked back.

I also still carried my real estate licence and worked that with pride for many years to come, right up to retirement. Two jobs were nothing unusual for me. We closed the deal on our new home and moved in with plenty of room to spare.

I did not expect to love this house but I did. It was great for the kids with plenty of space and everyone with their own room. The kids settled in and began to flower in the new environment and the past seemed to me, to be passing. The future looked bright.

There were smiles on faces and harmony reigned. Friends came to visit and school marks improved.

The builder had finished off the basement in the raised bungalow with a 2pc bath, a large bedroom, a huge family room with deep windows and a fireplace. I had plans for this space. With some friends I added a strip kitchen and a shower and it was ready to be rented. I felt I needed a little financial security after all that we had gone through. We got an excellent renter and things just fell into place at least for a while.

Our tenant was not used to kids and I had three, creating a slight problem.

Surprise:

About this time I received a call from my ex, which in itself was very unusual, for we never spoke.

He asked if we could get together to discuss something or other. I am not sure exactly how that conversation went after all this time, however we made arrangements to meet at a restaurant and we talked face to face, for the first time in years. It felt very strange.

It appeared that he had awakened from his day dream regarding his new mate and discovered that her blue eyes were cold, they held no warmth. She was not, who he had thought she was. Things did not seem to be working out. Did I have any thoughts on the matter?

Honestly, I cannot remember what I said. Hopefully I did not voice all my thoughts on this particular subject. I do remember the outcome however. What I had dreamed of in the beginning years before, just might come true.

He wanted to come home. What was I to do? What did I really want? How did I feel?

There were so many questions that were flying around in my head that I myself was spinning.

My renter had given notice and was leaving for a quieter lodging. The apartment was going to be vacant. Thanksgiving was coming up and it seemed like a good idea to bring their father home and see how things turned out.

I personally did not know what It was that I wanted after all these years. To put it bluntly, I was a little confused.

I was seeing a really wonderful man at the time and was unsure if I wanted to give that up, but in all honesty, how often do we get the chance to perhaps make things right and the kids deserved this chance.

I could not turn my back on that. It would be wrong to do so.

I said he could move into the apartment and we would tell the children that we were going to be friends, just so they would not get their hopes up, for nobody really knew what was about to happen.

It seemed like the safest thing to do.

He agreed. I believe the time frame was approximately 3 years practically to the day when he had left, so there was much to consider and perhaps too much time in between.

We would see.

Life had continued on after he had gone and I with it and quite honestly, I was not the woman he had known. I was someone entirely different.

I had grown up and I liked who I had become. That was never going to change. Just to keep things clear for me, this is what I wrote, trying to figure it out. I called it, **"Once Upon A Wish"**

<u>Once Upon A Wish</u>

I must search for my life and when I find it I must live it.
I have been granted the rare opportunity to search the ashes of the past,
For an Ember still burning with Life.
If I find it, I must carry it carefully into the
present, With Hope or is it Fear?
I need to do this because it is Right that I should …
or is it? This is what I must discover.
One day a long time ago …. We loved one another.
Can this tiny light, with its' puny warmth, be fanned into a flame
That will bring not one but two … into the future?
Whether or not this frail foundation,
Based on Memories of what once was …. And
mixed with experience …, not shared,
Will have the Strength, the Courage, the Constancy or even the Desire,
To find the Truth that now exists …. I do not know.
I only know that I must Test this.
I do know that I am Scared and Confused and a little Numb.
That my Emotions are chaotic … and that I am running.
That the memories are beautiful,
Yet distorted by a Pain, I never wished to feel again.
For I am Remembering.
Once there were five of us that lived, laughed and trusted together.
There are four that survived …. And we are heading for Home.
I have only two choices.
I must either go back and bring him with me …
because it is Right that I should,
Or I must step forward … Alone … with no
Regrets for the past I have known.
I must have asked for this Opportunity… for it has been granted me.
I need to see clearly, I need my friends near me.
I ask you to stay … God's Will be done in
my Life …. Always I Pray! (smc)

After 3 years he returned

As friends we spoke to the children and just prior to thanksgiving he came home and moved into the basement apartment.

It was awkward. He didn't communicate and pretty much remained in his own space. His non action was confusing to me. I mistakenly believed that it was up to him to help breach the void and build the bridge, to connect, to explain, to figure it out. He did nothing. I have no clear idea as to why.

My reality was that the man I had trusted with my life, above all others, had tossed me away as if I had no Worth. All that I Believed and all that I stood for, had been discarded like yesterdays' trash, and yet the worst harm done was to his children, by his neglect of them. He had pretty much disappeared from their lives for a few years. There had been moments spent with them but nothing substantial, nothing they could relate to or hold onto or believe in. Was this now his concept of Love?

Certainly all this needed to be addressed. I had watched them suffer the neglect with my hands tied. Did he not understand this?

Over time I had learned that it was a natural transition for a child deprived of love, affection and security to transfer those fears, that pain, into anger against the parent that remained. I was that parent. I took it on. A child instinctively knows that no matter what they did, the parent that stayed would always be there, loving them. Of the one gone there was no such faith and to that missing parent, they gave, and gave and gave. Their goal quite simply was to be loved and who could blame them.

This had been a hard lesson for me to learn and yet with comprehension came clarity. There was much that we needed to talk about, he and I and yet as strangers now, he remained silent and with that silence I rebelled. Rebelling is something that I do, it's called Self Defense!

Bottom line, he came home. He never said he was "Sorry" for all the pain he had caused. He never asked for "Forgiveness", which I had already given. I truly believe that he had absolutely no concept of what had transpired during his absence. For an intelligent man, he was clueless. **I did not Trust him, I did not Respect him and I realized, finally that I did not love him.**

Love Died. He never even tried. How terribly sad. If anything, I feel so sorry for him and his limitations and all that he has lost.

Note: *a short time ago speaking to my grown up son I said," Your father is only doing the best he can. That is all he can do. That it falls so short of what is needed is beyond our control. He can do nothing more." It's up to you to accept this simple fact and give to him the love he needs and lacks." It had taken me many years to understand this.*

After we decided that we no longer worked and my ex left, I was an emotional basket case. It felt like failure all over again. It was what was necessary but not what I had wanted for my children. I hoped beyond hope that the children would be ok with us not being ok. At this point I did not know the answer to this question.

In the meantime I was dealing with my old friend, my rotten back, which attacked me with a vengeance. Once again my mind did not break, my body did. I was laid low, consigned to bed rest by doctors' instructions with pills I did not want to take. My life was on hold. I was angry, frustrated, sad and relieved that this part of my life was over forever or have I spoken too soon?

The final papers, I had forgotten about them. Stumbling to the washroom from a drug induced sleep, I passed out on the bathroom floor, hitting the edge of the counter on the way down. The next morning I looked in the mirror to find a swollen lip and a very ferocious black eye. My hair was, Scary! There was no smiling face in the mirror that day. What an absolute mess.

The doorbell rang and I moved slowly to answer the door. I did not care what I looked like. Standing there was a complete stranger who asked who I was and then handed me a large sealed envelope. It was the final papers.

I had just been served with Divorce Papers! For some unknown reason I had never thought about that. It hadn't take my ex very long after leaving, just a couple of weeks to get that job done. Stunned, feeling a little shaky, I just sat there holding them and looking at them and thinking, what a total waste of time all those 18 years had been with him. We had come down to just a few typed pages nullifying our existence together, and those papers, were then presented to me, by a stranger.

I did however have three priceless gems, my children. Each one a treasure and they were mine!

I didn't try to justify any of these thoughts! I was devastated.

My next thought, totally off the wall, had to do with pride. I need to tell you once again that I am not perfect. I remembered what I had looked like in the mirror this morning and the server at my door must have agreed that no man should have to live with that. How unfair. How totally unfair, circumstances can be. I would much rather have been all dolled up and looking adorable. Silly really, but I am, after all, only human.

<u>The Door</u>

I close the door softly behind me, on the life I knew before,
I cannot go there anymore.
The time has come to say goodbye.
To leave behind tears that have dried.
To forget promises made, but not fulfilled...
To Treasure the Beauty, that I remember still.
The door clicks smoothly into place,
And I know that I must leave this place.
There is no Peace here, nor will there ever be.
The gift of Love we shared is beyond repair.
I wish it were not so, but I can sorrow no more.
And we stopped believing in us.....long ago.
The door stands a silent testament, of what we cannot forget.
Immovable as our Stubbornness and useless Pride.
As strong as our anger, as deep as our pain.
Can something called Love, Remain?
Forgive me for not believing in you.
Accept that for me,
Your actions equalled our Truth. (smc)

CHAPTER 16

So I let go finally, totally, of all that had gone before. My life with him, gone forever and now I knew that I wanted it so. There were no more questions, no more doubts.

I pushed clear and moved with confidence knowing nothing would ever draw me back. I was done. I was free. Bursting Bubbles, pop, pop, pop, floating all around me sparkling in the sun.

My children deserved so much more. As a parent, it would always be my right and my privilege to provide for and protect them to the best of my ability.

I picked up the gauntlet and walked without fear towards our future. Mistakes would be made but were never intentional and from a distance I can now forgive myself, for being only human.

"Sorrow No More"

Let it go, just let it go. Let it drift behind you.
As each new path appears
Say goodbye to tears that never dry.
Take the time to Heal … Try.
Let it go, just let love go.
Let it blow off the edge of the storm.
Let pain fade and hide your face no more.
Smile and soon your heart will know
That it has wings on which to soar.
Let Love go and sorrow no more.
If love hurts and sadness rules your days,
And tears are never far away,
The Love is wrong, walk away, be strong.
Save your heart for a heart that cares.
Reach within, dig deep, win.
Let love go, just let it go,
And sorrow, sorrow no more. (smc)

CHAPTER 17

I realize you must have been waiting for me to come to my senses over this, **"I still love him,"** statement and I do apologize for taking so long.

You see I had always believed that marriage was forever and that was how I entered into it. Not everyone makes it and I realize now, that sometimes it is wrong to try and hold it together.

I had in all innocence, unknowingly, placed my husband on a pedestal right from the beginning of our life together and no union can move forward under those conditions. We are only human after all. Perfection is just someone else's dream of what we ourselves can achieve. A union must be based on equality and I unwittingly had placed myself in an inferior position.

Perhaps he believed that I was, inferior that is. As young as I was I was unaware of the mistake I had made, yet without mistakes we will not learn and we do not grow. It is only in asking my favourite question, "why" that I began to see what I had done wrong.

Please understand that I am not making excuses for him concerning his children, for there are none, none whatsoever for that.

A good friend of both of us told me after he had gone, "that he was only as good as he was, because I believed in him.' Trying to live up to that must have been hard for him. Perhaps I had expected too much and he being a proud man was not into failure. MY husband got caught up chasing his dreams and when they didn't seem to be coming true, he was lost. It could happen to any of us.

Did he choose the right path? I don't think so. There were so many repercussions from his wrong decisions and yet the children and I made it through. The road was rocky, the mountains we climbed high but the journey was one of learning and healing and as hard as it was, it made each one of the four of us left, stronger than we could ever have imagined.

My boys are amazing fathers, naturally, as they give to their babies all that had been missing in their own lives. Their children will not suffer any neglect and their lives will be cushioned with love. My daughter holds her daughters close to a loving heart and they have flourished within that warm blanket of love and security.

I am so very proud of all my children, having watched each one of them struggle with their own insecurities and overcoming them one by one over time. My babies, now grown, are amazing and I love them with all my heart. They are my greatest treasure and their children, my joy.

There is life after "Charlie, Rose, Sylvia, Ross or whoever." Our own life should never take second place. Remember and never forget, I matter, you matter, we matter .... No matter what!

<u>Note:</u> *We as parents need to remember that the* **Children Matter Most**. *Always protect the innocent.*

"The Eye of The Storm"

The thunder roars and crashes and booms, as lightning
rips jagged slashes thru darkened sky.
A Child races blindly in the forest below, **Lost …**
Alone … Confused … Afraid.
The storm rages and swirls about him. A cold rain
soaks the earth, turning the path to mud.
Tiny feet slow, bogged down in slippery soil.
The Child falls and does not rise.
Cold, **S**oaked to the skin, **E**xhausted and without
Hope, healing sleep, envelopes him.
The wind howls, branches bend, leaves fall upon the little body below.
The coloured tapestry keeps him warm. The
Love of God, surrounds him.
The **"Storm"** moves on …. **Unaware** …. Of the **harm done.**
Peace returns to the forest. Starlight keeps
watch, on the boy through the night.
As always … after the darkness … there is **light.**
A **M**iracle …. A **G**ift given … a **N**ew day.
Birds sing in branches high, drops of rain, slide down tree trunks wide.
A squirrel chatters by his side. The **"child'**
awakes, sits up, rubbing his eyes.
The leaves scatter. **Hope through Innocence …. Survives**.
He stands, stretches, reaching high, then follows the sunlight dancing by.
He reaches the edge of the forest, the meadow lies
before him. He skips, he runs, he slides. (smc)

A **Child** caught in the … **"Eye of the Storm"**, any
Storm … from (**Forces Within or Without**)
Deserves the **Miracle of Love** … to come through
it, **Intact, Healthy, Happy, Safe, Alive.**
A **child** is a **Miracle** full of **W**onder and **L**ight
Given to us to **Nurture** and **Protect**, keep **Safe,**
<u>"Not Neglect."</u>
We as Parents are the, **<u>Keepers of the Light</u>**. To keep
them **S**afe, is their **<u>"God Given Right!"</u>**
Lest we Forget …. Lest we ever Forget…

CHAPTER 18

I want to thank you for hanging in there as I took you on another tangent. Know that your Patience, overwhelms me!

I invited you in, not to display to the world my weaknesses or failures but to let you know that you are not alone and there are others out there walking through the shadows, searching for the light, who totally understand how hard and how scary your particular journey will be.

This will be, when all is said and done, a great adventure with you as the writer, the creator, the editor and the publisher. You are the one with the Power to rewrite your future. There is nobody that can do it better than you for you will be following your own Truth. Honesty matters. It is so very important to be totally honest with yourself. As you discover just how wonderful you are and you begin to use your God given talents, you will set free the person you were always meant to be. This journey that you didn't want to make, will be the journey you never wanted to miss, if you want it to be.

Of course, no two journeys will ever be the same. Mine will be so very different from yours and yet we are a family of Survivors, fighting many of the same battles but under extremely different circumstances.

Our backgrounds are different, our support systems are different, and our nationalities may be different. We will not all have jobs we can rely on or family and friends who are willing and able to help. Some of us will not have things like Courage, or Health, or Faith or even Confidence. There could be language barriers, or abuse issues which are monumental. There are so many issues that you may be facing that I do not understand or have to face, but never for one second forget, that those that travel through this uncharted and oft times dangerous and lonely road are fighting just as hard as you are for, **"The Right to Happiness." It's called the good fight.**

You need to know that there will be good days to lighten the load and make you strong and those, intermixed with the Bad days will lift you over the hurdles you face. Be not afraid. You are an army of one, fighting like the trooper you have become.

Remember, nobody is allowed to treat you badly or put you down, not ever, it is not allowed. While the battle surrounds you, do not lose your sense of self.

I will give you an example of one of my good days. It's a perfect summer day, near Cameron ON. A friend shared this beautiful piece of earth with me. I know you are dealing with many factors right now but always, remember to breathe. The beauty that surrounds us will lift us up beyond every day cares, strengthen our resolve and bring us peace. It will make strong, our strength. I call this **"The Magical Forest."**

"The Magical Forest"

I stepped out of the suns' light and into a world of shadow.
Silence fell softly upon my head.
It lay lightly upon my shoulders, it burrowed deep into my heart.
Without sound, I moved forward into the forest.
I walked upon a carpet of warm earth,
Dusted with fallen needles and mixed with seasons leaves.
The path I followed wandered wide and flowed gently,
Softly rising then tumbling slowly,
Hugging the contours up the knolls and down
as if the Earth itself were breathing.
It licked and lapped like ocean waves the border
of guardian trees that edged its' journey,
Pushing, nudging, stubbornly … refusing to give way.
Trees like giant sentinels stood proud, tall,
straight, in row upon cascading row.
Their branches swayed and touched and talked to a playful breeze,
That jumped from limb to limb and back
again. Trees with breeze … danced.
Daylight spilled infrequently and without prejudice
through tiny openings in Gods' canopy of trees.
It slid down the sides of heavy rippled bark,
Filtered through green laced ferns,
…… Sat upon the rotted stumps ……
Entranced I continued to walk,
Lured by the constant and ever changing beauty of the magical forest.
I was still in my world but the world had stopped
moving. … It sat hushed and waiting.
The suns' light beckoned. A few more steps and
I would once again be back in chaos.
I wrapped the Peace I had found like a cloak
about me, and stepped with Strength,
…… Back into my Life ……
The Journey Continues …. With Hope I embrace it. (smc)

A little advice, perhaps not wanted but definitely beneficial. Spread your wings. Take the time to fly and fly high. There are no limits to what the human experience can be or should be. It is entirely up to us. Get involved, stay involved, try new things, open up the possibilities. Make the time. In the course of my journey as I stopped to breathe, I realized that I was alone and desperately lonely. I made new single friends, cherished my forever friends and always there was family. I was fortunate.

I decided that my life should not be a continuous battle for survival. I rediscovered the joy of dancing. The music lifted my spirits, the movement released the stress, positive endorphins bounced like bubbles bursting, pop, pop, pop. I found myself smiling. It had been so long, too long and it felt great to feel normal. For long hours into that first night I danced.

I became a free spirit with no restrictions. The movement and the music made me feel young and carefree once more. The feelings were incredible.

Instead of standing alone on life's highway watching the traffic passing by, I jumped in, kicked up my heels and had some fun. It was long overdue.

It became a regular pastime of mine. Strangers that I didn't know set their watches by me. One night as I walked into the room, three men standing about said, "I guess it's 10:45 pm, here she comes." Startled that my movements had been noted by these strangers I continued into the room.

On dance night, after the children were settled I would set out. I usually ran into the train passing at the crossing near where the dance was held. I had no idea that my timing was a set pattern. Walking in alone was never easy but nobody ever knew how scary it was, for I walked in with attitude, you know, fake it till you make it. I would scout the room for my new single friends.

When I first went out nobody would ask me to dance. What was wrong with me, I wondered? I watched as young women and older women and tall and small and pretty and plain were being asked to dance, but never me. I was passable, cute, well dressed, slim. I later learned that posture alone, sends out specific codes for anyone who might be watching.

I was sending out negative vibes, **"Beware, Unavailable, Do Not Touch! Go Away, Fragile."**

All of these things were true. I had come to dance and so I danced with my new girlfriends. The fast dances. It was great fun, great exercise and a total stress reliever. I danced up a storm and let loose. It was good for me.

Complete strangers would come up to me, both men and women and say that they loved to watch me dance. I was totally surprised. One man started by saying, "I don't want to dance with you" which threw me totally off balance, until he continued, "I just love watching you."

Months later a man I was dancing with said to me, "the first time I danced slow with you I couldn't wait to get off the dance floor, you were like an immovable stone wall."

Well that was brutally honest, but honestly he was probably correct.

I had only ever danced with my husband and been close to him and I was vulnerable without realizing it. I was totally uncomfortable with a stranger holding me.

His statement explained a lot of what I had not understood about myself and exactly where I was, on my road to recovery. Not far, barely there at all. Locked in memories.

This particular man was a great dancer and we became friends and we danced often after that. I also discovered that those that could dance looked for matching dancers. I did too. It was so much more fun dancing with a partner that could exactly match you step for step.

It was like floating on air. With such a dancer I would be smiling all night long.

CHAPTER 19

I want you to know that I found a new world, new friends, new activities and something that had been missing lately, Hope. The singles group, men and women became to me a family of friends. Our own particular group of friends were strong and their values matched my own.

We planned vacations together, and would spend holidays like Thanksgiving together for there were many that were not as fortunate as I and they had nobody to spend these special times with. We supported one another and there were strength in numbers.

We went to the same venues in our own time frame, coming and going but there was always someone there that we called friend.

If someone of questionable character approached one of the girls the men of our group would give us the nod, yes or no. They watched out for us. Ultimately it was up to us to choose who we got to know but it was good knowing information that might be required to keep us safe.

Over time our border of friends grew and one such friend befriended my kids.

In all honesty, their own father was pretty much absent from their lives at this point and I wanted to fill that void if possible. In this case I made a huge mistake.

This man embraced my family. I think that he was missing his own children. As it turned out I should never have let him get close to mine.

He was not real and one day, he just disappeared. I had no answer as to why to give my children.

My son was hurt once more and again there was nothing I could do to stop the pain. What I witnessed is what I wrote.

I called this "My Fatherless Son."

"My Fatherless Son"

A young boy with dark tousled curls framing a sweet little face, wanders aimlessly on the stone slab patio of his borrowed home. The sun is shining and the background of dense trees running down to surround the creek make his playground a haven for most little boys. Yet there is no sunshine in his eyes and his mouth refuses a smile. His young frame, football broad, is gangly now as he stretches to fill his advanced age. Eleven is all.

The basketball that fills his child's hands, bounces periodically up and down, but he does not try for a basket. Perhaps he does not believe that he can. He does not believe in anything and there is little heart left. Shoulders slumped, head down, there is no confidence in his step. No joy.

He comes once again to the door and asks if "J" has called. "No." I said. "Right', says he trying to be strong, and shrugging his tiny shoulders he walks away. A tear runs down his cheek and disappears in the fist of his hand. I watch, heart breaking and helpless to help. I ask myself the age old question, …why?

My son, mostly fatherless since eight, had found a friend, a best friend, that is what he had told him, almost a dad, or rather this man had found him and played with him and worked with him and loved him in every way, every single day, for quite a while. This man had chased the shadows away and brought laughter and joy, to this one small boy … my youngest son.

I guess it was too much to ask of any man, that he continue to see my son. I guess it was too much to hope for, that this stranger who had become a friend would allow a friendship of such importance not to end. Isn't life strange, strange and cruel that one so small should walk without hope, without joy. I was only a mom and I could not fill this void.

It has been my observation that some men are just little boys, playing with their toys, there for the good times, unable to find the strength for the bad. They profess to know what love is, but it's just a whim and no one really wins. They forget what truth is, if they ever knew. When the sun is shining they shine and with the rain … they run.

The stranger that became our friend, sadly was one of them. I thought he was different. I was wrong. I believed in him. It was wrong that I did. I trusted him and he surrounded us with pain. My love and my assurance will not change the sadness in my little boy's heart, for no one can replace his **Best Friend** "J".

I am feeling anger now and that is good. I will give strength, love and truth to my little boy. He will be a survivor just like his mom and he will make me proud. God is Love, the Ultimate Love we can believe in. We will believe. In the name of love …… (smc)

Note: *Obviously these events were after my ex-husband's and my attempt, such as it was, at reconciliation. Undoubtedly, it could have been one of the main reasons why I allowed this man to get close to my children. The best father for them would be their own but a substitute perhaps was necessary.*

CHAPTER 20

<u>The Next Step:</u>

So I moved on to the next step. I was now free. Divorced, lonely and looking for someone special just for me. I believed that I was ready. For the most part my children were minus a father. We all deserved something better. And so my search began. I was looking for quality, sincerity, gentleness, honesty and integrity. I wanted to laugh again and not be sad. Was that so bad? I needed to be held and valued and understood. I needed to be loved. I wanted someone who would embrace my children and let them know that they were special and worthy of love. I knew that they were. It seemed however, that my loving them was not quite enough. I needed them to be happy.

I took a step into the scary world of singles searching for a life mate and a father figure for my children. It took a leap of faith, with courage not far behind. I would put my heart on the line, hoping beyond hope that those I met, would not let me down and that there would be no pain.

Of course that would turn out to be nearly impossible, for anything of value there is always a risk. I took that risk.

Unfortunately, Trust Issues were and are still huge to me, but bypassing that I would take a chance once again on love. I no longer trusted blindly, instead I knew now, that Trust must be earned. No gimmes on that one.

As I journeyed alone into this unknown world of dating and realized that I would have to get close and personal, I left behind for always, my fairy tale beliefs. I now had a list of requirements necessary for stepping out of my comfort zone.

#1. Attraction mattered, superficial or not.

#2. I searched for those with hearts that knew how to use them. (no heart, no go.)

#3. I wanted strength mixed with unique personalities.

#4. Intelligence mixed with wisdom was important to me.

#5. A sense of the ridiculous and the ability to laugh at oneself was vital

#6. A team player would be great. I knew I needed that.

#7. A non-smoker, (definitely).

#8. Occasional drinker was ok. I myself never did.

#9. A man that loved his children was major. It meant that he was capable of loving mine.

#10. I noticed men of my age were slowing down and I needed someone who could keep up with me.

In other words, flat out, I had a plan but I found for me …. Romance was not far behind. I realized that I would have to care, or I would not go there. Love mattered.

Each choice I chose over time, met my criteria, yet they were all uniquely different. For each person of worth that I got to know, there was something about that individual that I found to love. I have never regretted, not once, the love I gave nor was there ever a time that I did not value the love I received.

From some I received complete acceptance, a sweetness of nature, a sense of fairness. Some believed in who I was and all that I would accomplish. They made me stretch my wings and fly. Others trusted me and opened up their hearts to allow me to see their vulnerability. They felt safe with me, enough to share with me their story.

It's called caring and I began to understand the very fragile rope that some of us clung to, as with shaky steps we took a chance on getting to know one another.

I know that we each asked ourselves the question, **"Is this the one?"**

There is no easy answer to that question.

No matter how strong, or intelligent, or how big our hearts, we are all in some small way, vulnerable to life and its challenges and tragedies. It did not mean that we were unlovable or undeserving or not strong. It actually meant that sometimes, Love, cannot triumph over a pain too deep or scars too gruesome. Sometimes love is not enough. I learned this first hand.

Circumstances that we may know nothing about can leave the victims of tragedy or trauma or abuse, believing that life can never get better and they themselves are not deserving of happiness.

Their life taught them that. What a hell of a mess. How can someone travel beyond that?

Even if we know all that went before, those that we love sometimes never make it back, no matter what we do. Sadly I know this to be true. With this in mind I wrote: "**Undiagnosed Insanity.**"

<u>Undiagnosed Insanity</u>

It's a rare disease not easily detected,
The patient appearing normal, walking, talking, working, playing.
It is only when he draws near and interacts and then reacts,
That the symptoms appear and the confusion begins,
For it is then, that he walks in fear.
He appears confident, strong, sure, his intellect is superb.
Yet he is insecure and his understanding nil,
for he does not know, what truth is.
The cause is trauma and pain so severe, it severs the connection forever,
From heart to soul to brain, and the patient is never quite the same.
The candidates for undiagnosed insanity are from the crème of the crop.
The very top of humanity, those who once had hearts,
And someone, somewhere, made those poor hearts
bleed, leaving them alone in dire need.
They are the faithful and the true, those that
trusted and had compassion,
And someone, somewhere, broke that sacred
trust to feed their own selfishness.
Trust turned to distrust and compassion disappeared,
And the patient himself, sat in judgment upon
all those who appeared, after the pain.
Forgiveness was not something that came easily or even at all,
And all the love and care, once so freely given, was
driven underground, till there was nothing there.
Those that cared were frozen out, by this poor
broken heart, that time did not repair.
To love them only causes pain and yet they
must have love, their life to sustain.
The Tragedy is, that they cannot live with reality,
And that my friend is the definition, of this malady.
The only sure cure is Love and that is the one
thing, they can no longer believe in.
In vain we try to reach. …. Those that we love. (smc)

I know a beautiful man with an amazing heart, who cannot accept the fact that he is totally loveable. Instead he is caught in a vortex that continually carries him back to his childhood. A mothers' love should have supported and protected him. Instead her own anger and pain destroyed his innocence, took away any chance of happiness and left him defenseless. His story is not mine to tell, know only that he suffered greatly from neglect and terrible abuse in many forms that should never have been allowed. As time passed, others in his life let him down until that is all that he knew, that was all that he saw and all that he felt.

At one time I must have been one of them. I knew him well and I believed in him always and told him constantly. It made no difference. At some point the abused can become the abuser, their take on life too fragile. They fight back, (**not the enemy that caused the pain**) but rather those that remain. In this case, looking back, I believe that he needed to test those he loved to see if they really cared. Would they stay? Abuse was what he knew and sometimes it was what he used. I know he never meant to.

Strange Silences

Strange silences surround me, confound me and I
find myself alone, shut out, as you shut down.
For some unknown reason, you believe that I should understand.
How could I possibly, when I am left all alone
and you are not there to explain,
The how and why of where you've gone?
I am lost, confused, afraid. I feel sure that somehow, I am to blame.
Tell me what did I do ... what is my shame?
The strange silences, leave me lonely and missing you.
Strange silences come swiftly out of the blue.
One moment you are with me, the next I am someone you never knew.
Where do you go? What is it that happens to you?
I reach out my hands to touch a man I cannot
reach. I call your name, you do not speak.
Shadows fall heavy upon my head. The sun's
light dims. Fear attacks my limbs.
Am I fighting a battle I cannot win?
All I ever wanted was to be close to you.
I wanted to know your ins and outs, your ups your downs.
I wanted your mind clear, your heart happy, your soul free.
I wanted to make a Difference .... I thought that you loved me.
Tell me where did I go wrong ... Please teach me, to be more strong. smc

Without warning I was up close and personal with my own initiation into the world of abuse.

I am a communicator, always have been. He shut me out as he shut down. The silence was deafening. I was totally confused the first time it happened. What was going on? What had I done? How could I fix this?

Can you see a pattern here? I had taken on the role of offender. I accepted that I was somehow at fault. I just wanted my sweet man back. Where had he gone and why?

In the beginning I didn't understand that his actions were abusive and yet I was reeling from it, confused and in pain.

Then because I loved him and knew his background I began to understand and I stayed. Over time I came to know that when the emotional pain became too great for me I should step back, withdraw to a safe distance to heal and grow strong once more and then step back into my life with him.

I knew instinctively that when he went, where he went he did so because he too was hurting. I did not know how to stop his pain. I knew his heart was good and so I stayed for a long, long, time.

Eventually there came a time when sanity must be maintained and I knew that I could no longer stay.

It was a cycle that never seemed to stop. We were happy and then we were not. And then we were.

I loved him then and when I finally left I changed that love to the love of a treasured friend.

Leaving was one of the hardest decisions I ever had to make, but I had fought too hard to be healthy, to lose that battle.

Many of us without first hand knowledge ask, "why do they stay, why not just leave?" Huge questions with many answers. Each answer is personal **and from a victims point of view.**

This man was a major player in my life and well worth loving.

His faith in his **"Right to Happiness"** was destroyed long ago when he was just a child. How terribly wrong. How terribly sad. How much I wish it were not so. In answer to my question" why" and for him, I wrote **"Driftwood."**

<u>Driftwood"</u>

From where did you come, on your journey to me?
How far have you travelled, what have you seen?
From what distant shore did you embark?
From what branch of which tree, were you torn apart?
All I see now …. Is your Beauty.
Tell me, were you storm tossed, rough handled, wave licked.
Did you bump along the bottom or was your journey quick.
Were you always alone, lost or in pain?
What are you feeling? What is your name?
I found you on the shore on a perfect summer day,
Wrapped in warm grains of sand, healing in the suns' soft rays.
My hands are gentle, my heart is strong,
I want to take you home where you belong.
Life's journey brought you to me.
All I see now … is your Beauty.
God creates Miracles for those who believe.
You are a Miracle, God gave to me. (smc)

CHAPTER 21

Hello again. That was a necessary detour. I needed to go off track, this time with abuse issues for they played an important role in my own personal growth.

Over time I found that I was continually learning, experiencing so many things that I had known absolutely nothing about. Some of the lessons were hard for me and yet I stubbornly refused to ignore what I had seen, and lived through and felt, for I knew it was all part of the human experience and now a vital part of my own reality.

For your information, **"sleeping beauty"** had awakened, and was gratefully letting go of her fairy tale existence. Her life had been too happy, too simple, too protected for far too long. Now, having tasted life as it was meant to be lived, with all its many challenges, dangers, possibilities and decisions, with mistakes waiting to happen and successes to be achieved, there was no way, that **"sleeping beauty"** was retreating back to **"safe!"** That destructive action would never again, come into play.

So here I was in the real world where there was no place left to hide and I had no desire to do so.

I finally understood that I was meant to make this journey from start to finish and I did not want it any other way. Where there was pain there would be the wonder of survival, mixed with unbelievable strength. Confusion would give way to clear vision as my mind began to play with a multitude of possible solutions. Choices were scattered all around me leaving me with no reason to fear, anything at all. Time would always be slipping away and so procrastination was not a viable commodity.

I knew that I needed to be happy and I would continue to pursue this elusive something. I began to see that happy, needed to start with me. So simple really. I had been happy many times before, why not once more? It was definitely worth searching for.

One thing I knew for certain was that I must not judge. I could try to help others but I was unworthy to judge them. It was wrong that I should even attempt judgement when I had not walked the paths they trod, knew not the trials and struggles they faced or the enemies, real or imagined that they fought.

Lessons Learned At Work

All day long I sit here doing my work and keeping an eye to the picture before me, enchanting, ever-changing and entertaining. As people come upon my window which reflects like a mirror, I watch, amused, to see what they will do.

They invariably do something. It takes a strong personality not to check out the perfection of self. Those who come to my window in the course of their day, see only the reflection of themselves while I notice their reactions to the self that they see.

My window beckons young and old and one by one they come. Is it vanity, curiosity, insecurity? Mothers with children running at their feet, pause and quickly take a peek hoping that nobody will notice. They smile or frown and quickly turn away, depending on what they see.

I have had ties straightened, skirts adjusted, hips swaying or swaggering, hair being flipped and occasionally and usually a man, will stand directly in my line of vision and pull out a comb for their hair. They are bold and unashamed and they like what they see.

This is pure vanity and no mystery and as basic and human as we all can be. I sit quietly and enjoy the view. Would not you?

Do the Dictates of Society and the standards of perfection that they set, present us with insecurities that can't be met? Are these insecurities so immense that we require physical proof of our right to acceptance by a world based largely on shallow?

Are those of us, blessed with passable physical beauty, grateful for that Blessing? Are we even aware that it is one? If so, I wonder how the less fortunate, the not fair of face, or perfectly graced, the ragamuffins, the mentally and physically challenged, the illiterate, you get the picture, how can they stand up and face the self- appointed Judges of Society who have displaced self -worth?

Ask yourself if you and I, who can safely pass the critical eyes of our self centered and shallow world need the reassurance of the looking glass, how do those not so blessed, achieve togetherness?

Would you and I survive with the odds stacked against us? Would we have the strength of character even to begin, with less than the perfection we have been given?

Perhaps during the course of our too busy lives, we should take the time to reflect on all the souls that we neglect!

Ask yourself if we steer away from the imperfect, impoverished, derelict? Do we frown upon or pass judgement on the babies who are having babies, or stiletto heels and tight little skirts, or the ragged old man who hangs out in the park, a brown bag not quite hidden under his threadbare shirt? Do we find ourselves criticizing the frequenters of the donut shops who look like they do not need that donut?

Snap judgements are part and parcel of our society and yet we do not look any deeper to discover the history of those we would condemn. In smug satisfaction we proudly hold up our head.

Faced with their lives, would we have managed better than them? Just thoughts, just wondering.

The paddy wagon is dropping another load of humanity outside my window. They shuffle along with hands and feet in chains and chins down. I often wonder just what circumstances brought them here. What exactly is their story and would it make a difference if I knew?

Always more questions. Do you have questions too? Are the thoughts we sometimes have, a form of unintentional abuse?

Once again I will ask you to wander with me, into the path of Abuse. Just to let you know, I faced abuse not once but twice on my road to happiness. I admit that both times the abuse came from those that I loved and I do know, that they loved me. Seriously, there is no doubt in my mind about that.

To both of these men, my love holds firm, changed only to that of a forever friend. I hope that they remember this and that somehow, (once loved and always loved) makes a difference in their own lives.

Abuse comes in many forms. Quite often the abuser is unaware that their actions are abusive. Many times it occurs because they have been hurt or were traumatized by some event beyond their control.

I realize that I am making excuses for, "**this wrong behaviour**" and yet I was there, I knew their history and understood the reasons for their actions.

Loving them, I chose to stay and to go on loving them as long as I could.

Note: <u>This is not something that I recommend for anyone else!</u>

Silence is one form of Abuse. **Criticism** and constant **put downs** another. **Isolation** is really rather scary for there is nobody to turn to for help, and that quite often, is the plan.

(I'm shouting here, "victims beware.")

Mind games can play havoc with your sanity. There are so many forms of **Fear** to be inflicted upon those that are defenseless and without hope. Know that **Accidents** can happen, yet most times recurring accidents are **not Self- inflicted**.

Bruises can be hidden and **Broken Limbs** explained but the **Scars within**, keep right on "**Hurting**." **Stalking** is a whole other kettle of fish. There is no excuse for **Temper or Anger** that results in **Physical Violence**. **Sexual Abuse** is not the **Right** of one human being over another.

Family and friends may be totally unaware of the "**<u>Plight of the Victim</u>**," whom they love, for the **Abuser** shows to the world a completely different and usually beautiful individual. In this regard, those that could possibly help, often turn away, for they do not **Believe,** that the Abuse is real!

Unless abused ourselves, none of us can really understand the massive damage that occurs to the Victim. To ask for help is most often not something the **Victims of Abuse** can do. This statement is true! They are afraid of repercussions and sometimes also ashamed, for over time they have come to believe that somehow they, themselves, are to blame! **This thought process is so very wrong!** The Victim should never be blamed. How do we stop the insanity? On the outside looking in, how do we approach it? Where do we even begin? I do know that the threats are real and the scars that are left, sometimes never heal.

"Shadows and Light"

Hello are you out there in the shadows, running scared?
Are you walking in the darkness?
I would perish there.
I need the world around me with its beauty and its pain.
There is so much to learn here,
So much to gain.
Each step that I am taking, will bring me closer still,
To the woman I am seeking
… me …
I just know it will.
Hello are you coming, I need to see your face?
Come and reap the blessings,
Earn your special place.
You need to meet the people that you were meant to know.
Let them understand and love you,
So you yourself can grow.
Sometimes my steps are weary, the load I carry great,
But with each challenge that I conquer,
My heart accelerates.
I find myself flying. I will not accept defeat.
There is a difference between the shadows and the light.
One is caused by fear … the other one is right.
I cannot fight your battles, nor conquer all your doubts,
I know only that I will miss you,
If you don't come out. (smc)

CHAPTER 22

So here I go to another chapter, as I searched to discover that someone special that I was meant to find. Let's start at the very beginning. I saw him standing alone in the doorway of a singles dance looking handsome, well dressed and rather shy.

I was intrigued. He stood apart from many of the regulars and I wondered who he was. I pointed him out to my girlfriend and she immediately said, "I bet he doesn't even speak English." I was startled, her statement was so wrong on so many levels and that thought never had crossed my mind. What I wanted to know was, is he going to come in? It looked doubtful. He was hesitant but he did.

I watched as he made his way around the huge dance floor looking a little out of place. I lost sight of him and the next thing I knew he was standing just two feet away. Wow! Our eyes connected and in perfect English, he asked me to dance. We danced the entire night and talked and laughed and at the end of the evening we were not ready to say goodnight. We had connected. It was effortless.

As the story goes, we sat talking most of the night. As we watched the sun rise on a perfect day he asked if I were free to get together and I, without hesitation, said yes.

A few hours later he returned and bounded down the back stairs to my temporary home holding an armful of red roses, which he gallantly presented to me. He was smiling. It had been so very long since someone had made me feel so special and being special to him lasted a long, long time, in fact many years.

He had two small children. His baby was only three years old and his son the age of my youngest one. I embraced them with all my heart for how can you not, love a child? It is just such a natural thing to do.

He himself was an only child with an adoring mother who believed that I was not quite pretty enough for her handsome son. She told me as much. I paid absolutely no attention to that and grew to love this extraordinary woman who was both mother and grandmother to his children.

His dad was a gruff old man who spoke little but played the mandolin beautifully with his huge rough- workened hands. He also taught himself to use the computer and somehow put notes together to make music. I have always believed that there was more than met the eye, with this quiet man that had provided so well for his family.

Needless to say our relationship was wonderfully happy for quite a few years and then problems crept in and some promises were not kept or were postponed. I thought that we could overcome them as time passed. What has love got to do with that?

Everything or so I mistakenly thought.

It turned out that it was not so. If you remember I have stated that Partners must be equals. Add respect and trust and throw in a large dash of love and what you have created should be wonderful. Right? Apparently, not always.

When raising children, parents must be united. They must stand firm and be the **"Adults."** The children should have borders, rules, consequences and be surrounded by love mixed with wisdom. That never happened and that was what destroyed my Faith, in our Relationship.

To this day I still love those kids, now grown, as if they were mine and I will always want them safe and happy.

I had never before met a man that was so very afraid of losing his children and with just cause. He would and did do everything to make sure that he could hold onto them and keep them safe.

For years he had battled with their mother, who knowing how much he loved them used the children as pawns to satisfy her wants, her needs, her ambitions. Fortunately the children were always his first priority.

When I first met him I was unaware of the ongoing battle that was raging and as time passed I became a witness to the insanity that was evident and realized how very wrong it was for the children to be exposed to this.

I now understood why the grandma was both mother and grandmother to his children.

At various times over the course of our years together, as I stood on the outside looking in, I clearly saw what motivated him.

The following will explain much better than I ever can.

"Their Dad"

Quietly he withdraws, unto himself.
Possessed of tremendous restraint, patiently he waits.
Steadily he draws from his greatest strength,
The Love that lives within.
Will Wisdom, Truth, and Honor, finally win?
The battle, if such it is, started long ago.
The Prize involved his children.
There is nothing in his World, more Precious than them.
No monetary value could ever replace, the sound of their voices,
The sweetness of their face, their young embrace.
His arms ache to hold them,
His heart breaks, alone, without them.
Yet he does not show his pain.
I see it only in the shadows of his eyes
And in the smiles, that no longer touch his face.
The scars of unshed tears,
Lie hidden in a heart that has been hurting for many years.
Helpless, loving them, I watch the tragedy unfold.
Should the children be told of this great Love,
That is theirs alone?
Their fathers' needs are few, he needs his children.
I believe they need him too. (smc)

**Now that we are all on the same page you can
begin to understand his actions.**

I believed then and still do today, that children need rules and
restrictions tempered by love. A child should never be the boss of the
household and yet that is what was happening to us. And he allowed it,
over and over again.

After a few years we went and bought a home together in a wonderful
area with enough room for all of our children and the plan in my mind and
heart was of course to move us all in together and live happily ever after.
This of course did not happen and apparently was never going to happen.

I had only my youngest son living at home with me at the time. The
house we chose was close to the schools they needed and I had volunteered
to drive them in the mornings. Three bedrooms were upstairs and the
rec room was taken by my son. It should have worked. I was happy and I
could see no problems. Lordy, Lordy, how old was I, that I still believed in
Miracles, for that was what was needed here?

In came the furniture from two different directions and our home
looked beautiful, but it never really became a home. Within the first year
our home was back on the market and I had given up. You know me the
believer, the stubborn one, I threw in the towel. I gave up on us.

His son never came. His beautiful little girl who had ruled his home
and his mothers' for her entire life was still pulling the strings and allowed
to do so. I did not then nor do I now blame this child for our problems. I
blame her dad for not believing in me. This statement is important. I will
give you an example of how our lives worked at that time.

We had invited friends over for dinner and to spend the evening. They were my best friends and I had prepared everything without a hitch, which was something for me. This was going to be fun. A half hour prior to their arrival with dinner almost ready for the table, his little girl decided she wanted to go to her grandmothers' house. I didn't agree. Her voice ruled.

Her dad took her over and I waited for him to return for dinner with our guests. We waited. He stayed with his daughter and never called. Thankfully my friends were surprised but supportive, and yet I was angry.

Perhaps I should tell you here and now that I hardly ever get angry. I was very angry that night. I suppose that this incident seems rather petty at the moment and if I had not been living it for so long, I would agree. Unfortunately it broke my heart and my spirit. I no longer believed in us.

To me this was major. I was never going to come first in anything and he did not trust me with his children. He has no idea how much this hurt my heart, even to this day.

The kids came first and then his mother had her say and always his ex would interfere and then maybe me and mine. My thoughts, my insight into the matter did not matter, not ever. It was over for me and it was time.

Did I still love this man? You bet I did! I had more trouble letting go of this relationship than I had my marriage which, when you think of it, is very sad. I felt closer to him than I had to my husband, for he had a beautiful and loving heart. Did I understand his actions? Yes I did. That did not however, stop the pain of his wrong decisions and I needed the pain to stop. I needed to make a decision.

<u>"Stay or Go"</u>

I ask myself day and night, night and day,
Should I go or should I stay?
Always love gets in my way.
If I choose to walk away, I lose.
If I stay as it is today, I've already lost.
How great is the cost?
Is it better to remain with you in pain,
Or stand all alone once again?
Do I value myself not at all?
Is this then, the reason I stall?
For surely it is a stranger that keeps hurting me,
Or a blind man, refusing to see.
I must choose my reality,
To stay with you, or be happy.
Yesterday can be but a memory.
Tomorrow a tragedy.
Today I live and die by my choice.
I must decide.   (smc)

CHAPTER 23

How does abuse come into this scenario?

The house that I loved went on the market and we stayed together until it sold. During that time he realized perhaps that some mistakes had been made and he tried to put it back together. His efforts were sincere. He asked me to marry him after we had broken up. He asked too late.

I no longer believed that it was possible to be happy in this relationship. My decision to say goodbye had taken all the strength that I had left. This loss was one of my greatest sorrows.

It left me feeling like a wet dishrag, limp, exhausted and with no Faith left in the possibility of us. My son went to live with his dad after this, which totally crushed my heart. My son was gone and my world no longer made sense. I was more alone now than I had ever been, totally and truly alone.

To compensate I went back out dancing, something that I loved to do and I began once more to live my extraordinary life. There were no other options.

Again I was starting over and open once more to the possibility of new beginnings.

One night at the dance I met a man who asked very direct and personal questions, he had an agenda. He seemed to be coming from strength. I liked that. Strong is good. He asked me out and I accepted. I felt good about my decision. Where does the abuse come in? Well here it is.

Abuse came in the form of "**stalking**" from my last, very long term relationship.

I knew I was being watched, my movements monitored. The phone was still ringing from him and it was a constant tug of war for my emotions and heart were still involved you see, and my answer to the question of a date with someone new, should have been **"No"**, at least till the dust had settled.

I analyzed it. It was just one date, what harm could it do? It might lead nowhere and I needed some space, some peace, and some fun. To enter into a new relationship, even a date was suicidal and totally unfair to this man that I had just met. Unfortunately I did not know this at the time of my acceptance.

As it turned out my first date with someone new should have been my last. I should have insisted. I did not. Knowing I was being followed, that my family and friends were well known, still I thought I could fool my ex and be home free. Wrong!

I asked this new friend to pick me up at my daughters after work and suggested that we go to the show in the next town for a change. He did not questions this. I thought we had made it safely without being noticed but I was wrong again.

After we parked and were walking towards the show holding hands a shadow appeared right beside me, walking along with us and in a loud voice started putting me down while addressing my date. I was in shock and I am sure my new friend was too. What a nightmare. Beyond comprehension.

Later, my date and I went and had a long talk and I apologized to him and told him what had been going on for almost a year. "**I am so very sorry for what happened,**" I said from the bottom of my heart. The entire incident was truly awful and I had no right to put someone through that. It was wrong that I did.

At the end of our conversation we both decided that we wished to see each other again. That was totally my mistake. How can you possibly build a relationship on a crumbling foundation that could explode at any given moment? You can't. It's impossible.

We didn't think about that and the stalking actions continued, until one day, totally lost and feeling helpless, I went into a police station and asked for help.

Sitting in a small office in front of a detective I began to cry and I could not stop. How had I ever let things get so very bad?

I explained to the detective, what was happening and how long it had been going on and that I was not allowed to go forward with my life. I told him that I didn't want my ex to be hurt, for we had loved each other very much. I stated that he was just confused.

I asked only for the stalking to stop and it did stop. I never knew until much later how this was handled, nor the repercussions to him. When I learned exactly what had happened I was truly sorry. I realized just recently that being sorry was never going to be, good enough.

There will never be a time when I will come to believe that he did not love me. I know that he did and in all honesty, although I changed my love to that of a dear friend, my love in a far different form remains.

Regarding this episode in my life that I will never forget, I wrote **"Stalked"** so that others in distress would know that there were agencies set up to help those in need.

"Stalked"

She walked, always with shadows. Searching crowds for a certain face, size, and shape. Holding herself ready for confrontations, at any time and in any place. She never felt relaxed. She never felt safe. She drove fast, checking the road ahead, the streets behind, the side roads converging, expecting to see a little car with a lone grey haired driver, slipping in behind her.

Her home was no longer a haven, the outer doors not always secured. Automatically, as she crossed the threshold, she turned and locked and double locked, and all the while it played upon her nerves, that those locks, had become **"her world."**

She lived on the second floor and felt much too close to the ground. She was always aware of the possibility of danger and there was no peace to be found.

She still met with friends, laughed and played, and all the time they never knew that she felt, Alone, Abused, Afraid, for these were not the emotions that she displayed. Nobody knew when or even if the Stalker would change his tune. Nobody knew where or if he would stop the Stalking and make his move, or just what that move might be, for he was Lost in his own, **"World of Fantasy."**

His car patrolled her work, her home, her family and her friends. The phone infringed upon her privacy. The buzzer shattered the darkness of the night, bringing her awake to helplessness and despair. He was always near. She knew that he was everywhere.

He knew when her blinds were open, when shut, who came to visit and when they went out. He knew what lights were on, in which rooms, at what time.

What did he want, when would he stop, and what would he do? The scary part was that nobody knew, least of all him, for he was **"Confused."** From Heaven to Hell, from Freedom to Trapped, she couldn't go forward, she would never go back. Finally she acknowledged that, **"she needed help."** In Humility she asked, <u>**"to have her life back."**</u>

On the outside looking in it is hard to tell where the Love stopped and the Nightmare began. All that we know is that the Nightmare must end, sometimes Tragically, sometimes Magically, but always hopefully, surrounded by friends. Remember, we have no Right to **J**udge or **C**riticize or **C**ondemn for we have not walked where the **"Stalked"** have been. So if you are out there alone with your thoughts, afraid of the sunshine, afraid in the dark, find the Courage to **"Right This Wrong ... Be Strong."**

Reach ou**t** your hand and pick up the phone. Someone will answer, someone will hear. We understand that the Dangers are real. We know of the pain, confusion, fear. You are not alone, Help is near. We stand and fight, for your Right .... **To Choose a Life of Your Own!**

For People Helping People CALL: The Police, Social
Services, Family Councillors, Shelters (smc)

CHAPTER 24

"Threshold"

I stand at the threshold of a new day, there is
only one person standing in my way.
That person is me, who else could it be?
There are many things that I have felt, heard, seen.
There are many places that I have been.
There are memories bitter and sweet, intermixed
with each friend that I meet.
With each meeting I have become strong,
leaving fear behind as I travel along.
For every decision that I make, for everyone I must leave behind,
I know that those choices are only mine.
I rejoice in the freedom of choice!
With eyes sharpened through the passage of time,
And a clear understanding of my heart and mind,
I move forward into this new day.
I grow older yet feel not the loss of my youth.
It remains intact within a heart that still believes,
And a mind that conceives messages that time leaves.
I am the accumulation of all the love I have ever known.
The result of every thought and action of my own.
There are no excuses, no not one, that I can
make for the woman I have become.
The final story that has yet to be written is mine,
As it has always been since the beginning of time.
I stand at the threshold of a new day,
I still have time to make the world mine. (smc)

There are defining moments not quite forgotten in our past that have shaped and moulded us. Moments that have set us on paths that we may never have taken. Moments that have vibrated us into awareness in millions of small and apparently inconsequential ways.

All those moments have led us to the here and now. It is not the sensational moments of our lives that we should cherish, but rather the small, quiet, private moments that touch the heart and lift the soul.

These moments may seem like mere commonplace, unimportant events or happenings, but I know that together, bit by bit they shaped and defined my life, as step by step I stretched into my world.

These lasting impressions blasted my mind into thoughts that mattered and ways of thinking and analyzing how my world worked and my reactions to that world.

Memories, unforgettable that's what they are, not regrettable, that's for sure.

You may be wondering how any of these moments and memories that each of us carry, could have an effect on what we are dealing with today. That answer would be, absolutely everything.

With each step taken from our earliest memories and every lesson learned, we have been building **"Our Character."**

Although we may have forgotten about us for a while, know that this is our "Solid foundation."

We are ready and able to face any given situation that may befall us. We are Strong. We have spent a lifetime building blocks upon which to stand, strong and sure and as near perfect as anyone can imagine.

Our memories are pockets of **"Precious Time."**

If we but seek out these moments we will find, food for the Soul and thoughts to free our minds. I ask you to think back to the moments that impacted your life choices and from that, the roads that you have travelled. It is all part of your personal journey.

Whether or not you know it, you have arrived, you need only to remember these simple facts.

We were speaking of memories, mind altering moments since the beginning of our life, that have impacted our journey. Here are some of my defining moments, my building blocks, my firm foundations.

CHAPTER 25

Back to earliest memories …

It's summer and I am outside holding hands with my mommy and grandma. Clop, clop, clippity clop. Two huge horses pulling a wooden wagon, stop. A man with a wire basket jumps to the ground. Glass bottles carrying milk, with crème on top, clink together. The milk man drops them at grandmas' back door. Entranced, I watch. I'm nearly four.

Wonders in grandmas' garden. I raced into the back yard chasing my ball. It landed against the back of the house. Next to the ball I found the tiniest flower in the world with tiny green leaves and in its' centre a little white bell. I know it now as "lily of the Valley." So I set out to explore. It was not hard to see at the back of the garden against the white picket fence was a giant flower with a large yellow centre that stood like a tree towering over me. It's called the "sun flower". Walking back through the garden I saw carrot tops waving in the breeze. Squatting down I pulled real hard and a dirt dusted carrot is what I found. I dusted it off and took a bite. Hum, hum good. I like vegetables a lot.

I'm getting older and carrots were not the only tasty treat in the garden. I loved to eat plump juicy red tomatoes straight out of the dirt. Once started I could not stop. A terrific scold and home- made egg nog Is what I received, lots and lots to counter the effects of the canker sores I got. (I still love tomatoes but now they are washed.)

Grade 3:

High on a hill across from our house, I found a huge rock filled with gold, glistening in the sun, all sparkly and warm. With determination and much excitement and lots of pushing I rolled it down the hill to show my dad. We were rich! It turns out that it was only fools' gold, (mica) and nobody was impressed, but the rock stayed. It was too big to roll away.

Grandpas' house in Baltimore. It was farm country and I was a city girl. I met kids from the neighbouring farm and we ran together to their big old barn. It was all new to me. We climbed up the ladder into the hay loft. It was incredible. Sunlight came dancing through chinks in the barn board and mixed with dust motes of hay as we grabbed a thick rough rope hanging from a beam and like Tarzan we held on tight and swung from hay stack to hay stack and back. It was hilarious fun. We didn't need to spend money to have a great time. Friends and imagination were quite enough.

Young teen years … age 12 and 13

My parents and their best friends would go out at night when we were asleep. They never told us their plans. As it turned out I usually found out due to the fact that I woke up to discover their son who was fifteen and my secret crush, babysitting us. He was wonderful and let me get up to watch TV with him. At some point I started to wonder why I was waking up and then one night I saw him in my room.

As usual I got up and when it was time for me to get back in bed I didn't go back to sleep. He came in. I was a kid and he was a kid who was curious. Nothing much happened but it was weird and horrible to me. I remember yelling at him to get out. Now I realize he must have been scared to death at what his parents would do when they found out. Then it was all about me. Regardless, he never came again.

It would be necessary to say here that I was totally innocent of all things to do with me growing up into a woman. I knew nothing! This is not an exaggeration. I know that knowing nothing, would not be possible in the world of today, but my mom had not approached me on any of the things that were about to happen. The results were catastrophic to me. Here goes.

As usual I was running behind time getting ready for school and the others had left the house. I ran out of the bathroom scared to death and screaming that I was bleeding and I was going to die. It was only then that mom quietly took me by the hand and told me all the things I needed to know about that. She was prepared with everything I needed, she just hadn't prepared me. (Later the others got a book). I was definitely late for school that day and probably walking awkwardly up that long lonely hill. The cows no longer mattered. MY life was over and I was shattered.

I had no idea that we were poor! I had to be told by my friends next door. They must have thought that I needed to know. I believed that life was good, because it was for me. I thought when we had crackers under hot water with margarine and jam, that it was a treat. I do not ever remember being hungry. I guess being a loving and happy family made up for less money, or so it seemed then. Money today is not my priority.

"Daddy, I want to go to Church." I really have no idea where that thought came from but this is what I wanted. We were Christians but we never went. I was young and I was shy but I was also a little bit stubborn.

My parents loved me and so they said I could go and directed me and my little brother to the only Church in our neighbourhood. They did not accompany us on this our initial journey. We walked up that long, long hill and down the other side to a back street with a big church sitting neatly in the corner. I had just turned twelve and my brother was only eight and tightly holding hands we approached the door. Quietly we walked inside and stood in awe as the beautiful windows shone their colourful light across the pews.

There was a staircase and we went towards it trying not to be noticed. It seemed we had just sat down when this large shadow was in front of us demanding in an angry voice that we leave, that we were not allowed to be up there. From such a great distance of time it's hard to remember but I do remember that I was scared. We charged down the stairs and out into the sunlight, never to return.

When I told my dad what had happened he finally got involved and our family began to investigate different denominations of churches for us to join. We found the perfect one for me.

We lived in the last house on the end of our street, surrounded by open fields and encroaching country. I loved it. Something awe inspiring and eye opening and never to be forgotten was about to happen. We had rats in our basement and outside our back door. There was also an old wood pile at the back of our yard which contributed to our visitors, the rats. No, they were not sweet little mice.

Mom was furious and dad did not want to get involved so my Mom got some food with poison on it to solve the problem.

I sat safely inside on the steps to the back door and watched, entranced, through the screen to see what would happen next. Out of the many holes just outside the door, I saw the little rascals come out of their homes and zoom over to another hole and steal the bread that mom had spread all around. They were all scrambling to get as much as they could, stealing from each other.

Greedy little rats! The greed did them in. They disappeared, never to be seen again. I never forgot that lesson. Greed would never be my reality.

While at this house I learned many amazing lessons. There are no rocks filled with gold on the hill across the street. Don't look for it. Being poor didn't seem to matter, my life was good. I was someday going to grow up to be a woman. I could now handle all of that. Greed was a bad thing. I was 12. The world was opening up and it filled me with curiosity. What else was there left, I wondered, to discover? **I discovered that you never stop discovering**.

A New house, high school and me:

I was growing up with tons of new experiences ahead of me. I wondered what they would be. By now I knew that Life was exciting.

I was happy, confident, and not so shy. Our Church had a great program for kids and the kids I got to know were pretty fantastic. We had a class during the week called Seminary and each morning I would get ready, (I was a morning person which helped) and meet with friends for lessons. I loved my teacher. He was a very old man with tons of knowledge and I was a sponge that absorbed it all.

One of my favourite things about the mornings was the sunrise. It was glorious. The beauty of it filled my entire being and made me happy to be alive. After classes I was wired. I had been up for hours and when I hit the halls of high school I was beaming. A regular ray of sunshine. I was bouncing up and down the halls waiting for school to start. I was alert, energized.

All around me the students filtered in, dragging their feet, shoulders slumped, heads hanging low. My big smile and cherry hello seemed to frustrate them. When I grew up a part of me always remembered to search the sky for a sunrise and now I wait for the sunsets.

I learned early on that if someone didn't like me and I could not figure out why, I would greet them with a happy and smiling face and the end result would be, they either became my best friend or decided to leave me alone. One way or the other I was a winner. It was apparent to me that, **"it's hard to fight happiness."** I would choose to be happy.

In later years, I learned to channel this **"happy"** philosophy into a much needed weapon where my enemies were concerned. I never let them see any weakness or any pain caused. I would not give them that satisfaction. I gave them instead more love and sweeter smiles. It drove them crazy. They never knew what I was thinking or what I might do. It worked for me.

One of the most important lessons I learned as a young teen happened at a youth Conference in Toronto. Drawn to and standing at the fringe of a crowd of quiet teenagers, *(that in itself not natural)* I watched a teenage boy holding them all in thrall.

My very first visual reaction was that he was not attractive, so what exactly was the draw? Like a sponge needing an answer to the question of why, I waited to learn just exactly what there was about this young man that appeared to be so exciting to the others. As I listened to him entertain, talk, make us laugh, I totally forgot my first impression.

I no longer saw an unattractive boy, who was too tall and very skinny with a bad haircut and acne scarred face. I stood entranced watching a power house of intelligence, humour, and personality, who had total confidence in who he was. To find such strength in one so young was an inspiration to me. His beauty is what I saw.

I was probably around thirteen years of age and everywhere I looked there were lessons to be learned and I found that amazing.

I never forgot this particular lesson and many years later I related this concept of beauty to my two oldest granddaughters who are truly beautiful.

"Never forget that outward beauty is a Gift and it will make your life easier. Never, ever, abuse this Gift."

CHAPTER 26

Life was like a jigsaw puzzle to be explored, dissected, unravelled and put back together, but perhaps not always in the same old way. Life is complicated. I decided to keep asking myself the simple question, "why". It was opening up windows and doors to my mind.

I realized at any early age that I lived by my own set of rules, concepts, thoughts. In many ways I was young, naïve, untried. In many other ways I was ahead of my years. I was comfortable in my own skin. My thoughts always had a way of rearranging the events of my day, to fit into a pattern that I could accept. I had no problem with being on my own. I loved to lay on the grass down by the creek and listen to the thoughts that circled in my head, while birds circled overhead. On the other hand I seemed to have no problems interacting with my friends. Perhaps I was an old soul. Now I am just rather old.

Understanding me certainly is not a necessity for you. **How absurd that would be!** Understanding you however, is a whole different story!

You need to search out your own defining moments, your inspiration, and your strengths. That is what matters here. How do you think? Why do you do what you do? What triggers your reactions to certain buttons that rock your world? Is it possible for you to turn it around and come at it from a different angle? You are not a puppet on a string. You are the only one allowed to pull those strings. Do not ever give over control of your life to another. By that I mean your heart, your mind, your soul. These are Precious Gifts from God to you. You matter.

Remember always if you can, **to be kind!** If someone is making you unhappy, imagine just how unhappy that person must be. How sad for them! If it is possible, turn it around, pay it forward, make a difference, and yet realize, **"You are not responsible for their happiness."**

We are all linked together in some form or other at some time in the here and now or a future we cannot name. It's known as "The Human Condition," and we are all part of this. We cannot divest ourselves of the responsibility that each of us carries, for what we do and say, regardless of our intentions, will always have a rippling effect on those around us. Like the canoe in still waters, with the movement of the paddle we create a ripple and with the next pull, we have a wave.

Undoubtedly this will impact each of our lives in countless unknown ways. Action of any kind equals reactions and as we all react differently to those actions, like a tidal wave this can swamp us. We must individually, hold onto the memory of self for future reference, lest we forget, just who we are. Who we are matters greatly. Happiness matters greatly. Without this we could not survive. To not search for both would be a colossal waste of a Life! Do not let it be your Life. Something to think about.

There I go again, lost on the merry go round called internalization. Flights of fancy travelling through time to this particular page. It seems my mind and fingers search out my thought, regardless of my best intentions.

CHAPTER 27

Life is one wondrous, unexpected, beautiful and sometimes scary adventure that we were meant to discover. It has so many factions that we, as mere mortals may not have enough time left, to explore to our hearts content.

Sometimes Life is like a ball of coloured yarn, unravelling. You might ask how could this be when normally yarn is formed into a set pattern done with loving hands? I ask you to trust your imagination.

A playful kitten pounces upon the unsuspecting ball of yarn. As the ball falls to the floor the kitten follows. He stalks his prey and nudges it with his tiny nose. The coloured ball begins to roll. A furry paw swipes at it and the ball starts to unravel, travelling under couches, over slippers, around corners. It spins out of sight. On padded feet the kitten creeps. He discovers it once more as he slides on the shining kitchen floor. Playfully the kitten swats again and off the ball rolls. The ball is smaller now, its colours dim and finally it disappears leaving behind but a trail of string. The journey has been exciting, unexpected, not planned, spontaneous.

This ball of yarn was not forced into a "set pattern" by a **"Masters Hand."** It was allowed to run free as we ourselves were meant to be. How else would we learn and grow if not once, were we allowed to explore the great unknown. There is a place always for the "Masters Hand", but part of **"His"** plan is that we push the borders of our world and allow our minds to expand. Think of the possibilities.

I discovered over time that I had been wrong about so many things, but my mainstay, "love" came up for review. What I had always believed turned out, in reality, not to be true. Not always. I finally realized that sometimes, "love" is not near enough. There are too many variables intermixed with all those that we meet, for love of itself, to compete.

Those we find along life's journey are complex individuals searching just like us for a mate that matches the perfect picture in our mind. I ask in all sincerity, what if our picture is wrong for us? It does happen and unfortunately if we make a mistake about who we really need, we will once again, be confused. I met a man that had a plan and a map to follow to his heart's desire.

Much earlier, near the start of my nightmare, I wrote about a wonderful man that I was getting to know. We will call him (JCM), the year was 1989. I was very happy with him. He had a sweetness of spirit that gently touched my heart. He was an artist, an original, with unique ideas and he believed in me and my writing and felt strongly that I could do so much more. He nudged me to spread my wings. It was wonderful to be appreciated. We found we were in harmony about so many things as naturally we came together to explore the possibility of us. He was someone I could believe in. That was something rare for me way back then for as you know, Trust was the biggest hurdle I would ever have to climb.

Around this time my ex-husband approached me about coming home. This is what I had wanted for so long and the children needed their dad. I had to try. In sadness I talked to my friend and explained what I was feeling, (confused) and what I felt I needed to do. With doubts I said, Goodbye.

They say you can never go back and whether true or false, in our case this proved to be true for my ex and me.

I cannot remember why I never called back my friend. Perhaps I thought it was too late. I was unsure, scared and without confidence and I believed that I no longer fit the perfect picture in his mind. In hindsight I should have at least tried.

Picture Perfect

I had a picture in my mind of what I wanted, the life I'd live,
The people that would fill that life.
I set up rules and regulations and restrictions in my mind,
To achieve my heart's desire.
I refused to be diverted. I worked hard, I planned, I schemed.
My picture was clearer, closer,
Until I could almost see it, feel it, touch it.
I stripped away the last remaining bonds that
tied me to a life I never wanted.
I paid my dues.
I went out and searched for and found a mate,
Who fit the perfect picture in my mind.
We became the perfect couple, with the perfect life,
With no upsets, no diversion, no anger, no jealousy,
No hamburger, no pork and beans.
We worked when we should, laughed when we should,
Made love when we should.
We were as good as we could be. We were fitting together.
I am happy, I am sure that is what I feel.
After all, is this not what I wanted? (smc)

A piece of artwork from him had been placed in my mothers' mailbox for me shortly after the failed attempt to re-establish my marriage. I treasured it. I still have it tucked safely away for memories sake.

It is important that we hold dear all those that made our life, worth living. He was one of them.

As unpredictable as life can be, years later as I was telling a close friend about him, I went and pulled out his gift. It was then, way past the time when it could have mattered, that I discovered a hidden opening in the centre and within, were words written by him to me. How ironic.

Why now I wondered? Would it have been possible to take my life in a totally different direction? Now I am older still and many years have passed, but his friendship and his belief in me, is a memory I treasure. After that, each time I put pen to paper I remembered his faith in me.

He became the catalyst that spun me outward to search out life with all its' countless possibilities. He made me want more. His challenge has remained with me.

I wrote the following poem for him December 1989. This poem to date, is the only time I endeavoured to publish anything after countless years of writing.

A friend at work that knew about my writing told me about a poetry contest and gave me all the details. Out of all the words I'd written, how could I possibly choose what to enter? Which one should I choose? Understandably I decided that I would send in the poem about him. It was about two old friends coming together again.

I actually followed through and entered the "National Library of Poetry." Contest.

In September 1995, six years after our goodbye, I received a letter from the contest stating that my poem had been selected for publication in the forthcoming anthology under the title, "Shadows and Light". They enclosed an author' release form for me to send back. It felt really good to be acknowledged and yet as in many things, I got busy and put it away and forgot to send it in.

The poem was called **"As Always and Forever."**

"As Always And Forever"

Worn old slippers
Stuffed on tired old feet.
Torn and faded joggers,
Hugging the same lean seat.
Hair of a silvery hue,
Hangs rumpled, around eyes of blue.
There is still a decided shuffle.
When he walks.
And just a hint of accent,
When he talks.
With glasses perched
On the end of his nose,
He peers steadily towards the door.
I move forward into the Light.
And time rolls back.
With arms outstretched,
We reach one for the other,
Just two old friends,
Reunited and Together,
As Always and Forever. (smc)

CHAPTER 28

Due to the fact that someone that I respected and was close to, believed in me, I began to believe that I could accomplish more, and so I watched, I listened, I saw and I pondered.

Life was all around me and my mind absorbed what I had found. Sometimes from this I would write thoughts down that mattered to me. I needed to walk outside my comfort zone. I would give it a try. Samples of life as I saw it at that time, with clear perspective, are below. I learned that Life will always throw you curve balls to take you off course and expand your life experience. This would happen many times over. I needed to be ready.

<u>#1</u>

<u>I Hear You</u>

"I hear you,' she said to the Sweetheart of her youth, but she didn't speak the truth. She was busy baking bread and had not heard a word he'd said.

"Of course I'm listening, "she answered once again as she ran for the phone. "I'm here, I'm home," but all he ever felt in this house was alone.

"I'm coming", she said as he waited patiently, but she forgot about him and was lost to the story that she read.

One day he came home, head hanging low, shoulders slumped and feet dragging slow. They met at the door. "Something awful happened at work today. I need to talk to you right away." She stopped in her tracks, looked at him and said, "I understand, I'll just be a minute and I'll be right back."

He watched as she walked away. She never listened to a word he'd say. It seemed it had always been this way. He watched till she was out of sight.

The minutes stretched, somehow into hours, He was deep in thought. He took a second to look at the clock. His life was ticking away. He could no longer live this way.

He packed his clothes that night and stepped into the darkness of the night. It felt good and it was right.

She came home to find that she was all alone and on the table by the phone the Note said. "I hear you too and I also understand, but I am no longer waiting, I've done all I can."

As the words reached her heart, her thoughts echoed in the dark ..... "I'm listening Sweetheart," but there was no one to hear and the cold that she felt, was mixed with fear! (smc)

(A simple way not to have a relationship ..danger zone)

#2

<u>Rear View</u>

I took my kids to school today and driving home I
passed, another group of kids playing on the grass.
One little boy detached himself from the
crowd and walked toward the road.
I slowed down, but he did not cross ... He laid his
school bag down and dropped to the ground.
Drawing his knees up under his chin, his arms
went around them to hold them in.
He lowered his head and started to cry, I don't know why,
I watched him in my rear view mirror .... I had no right to interfere.
I will wonder about that little boy, all day
long. I will wonder where he's gone.
I will wonder if I was wrong .... To stand clear. The last time I saw him
He was crying ... in my rear view mirror... smc
(This was me not getting involved. I wonder how often this happens)

My youngest son grew up and joined the Canadian Armed Forces. Shortly after training and graduation these young people were called upon to perform their duties, in a land far across the sea. Below are this Mothers' thought and feelings, on what I witnessed and felt on the day they left.

#3

"The Journey"   (June 2005)

The sun rises high into a hot summer sky as the day of departure dawns. A young man, no longer a boy, moves forward into this day and says his Goodbyes, and then with purpose he turns and walks away. He is a member of the Canadian Armed Forces and today is the day he leaves, family, friends and homeland. Another Soldier joins him and another and another as they take leave of sweetheart, children, father, mother and friends. These men are friends. This is the very first journey to countries far across the sea, to lands of burning sun and sand and dangers as yet not faced and challenges yet to come.

As strangers in a strange land they come, to stand together, alone, in a place that is not their own. They are far away from all they have ever known. Strong of purpose, clear of mind, honorable, young, healthy and proud. Trained and yet untried under fire. May the fire not come. Who is the enemy and who is friend in a land where war has no beginning and appears to have no end? God above, please hold these Soldiers, close within the protection of your Love … in the Palm of your Hand … if you must. Give them the opportunity to do what they must, come what may. In God and these young men …. We place our Love and Trust. ……………..smc

One of my Son's best friends came up to me and
said, "Don't worry, I've got his back."
(Size doesn't matter, Heart does. He loved
my son. I felt better. He was safer)

My oldest son was expecting the arrival of twin baby boys. They came much too early to survive. How do you help with something like this? I opened up my arms and with love gathered him in. Below was what was written for the Funeral Service.

#4 : Morgan Douglas/Kaleb Kevin

On your journey to our World, a place called Earth, suddenly you both changed course. For reasons we do not know, or as yet, cannot understand, while we were dreaming, babies, God in His Wisdom, had other plans. One moment you were coming straight to us, and then were turned around. You were Heaven Bound.

You left us feeling, lost, bereft, alone, our hearts hurting, for the possibility of you and all the joy you would bring, was changed instantly to, only the wonder of what might have been. We held you for mere fragments of time, in the palm of our hands. So tiny, so delicate, so perfectly formed, and in those few moments we knew, the Miracle of each of you.

Heavenly Father called you home, to a place of harmony and peace and ultimate joy. He holds you close and He keeps you safe and warm. This is your "Sweet Destiny." Now your voices will blend with the Angels and you will play, together, among the stars. If we look we will see you twinkling a little brighter than the others, and we will know … that you are ours! We may see you jumping on puffy clouds, soft, thick and white, scattering pictures across our sky, or flying on the wings of Eagles in flight. You may fall asleep within the blanket that we know …. As Night. You can slip into our world on the rays of a sunbeam, or be the brightest flower in the garden and you can play and romp in the thunder of the surf, leaving your footprints in the sand, for us to follow. If we listen, we will hear you whisper in the wind, your music the rushing creek and the crackling leaves.

You have opened our eyes to the beauty of the Miracles that surround us. You will be within each Miracle that we find. We will keep searching for Miracles until once again, we can be with you. Keep busy our little Angels, using Heavenly Strokes to colour our world so never again will we fail to see the Magic, the Beauty, the Mystery of Life's infinite possibilities.

And so on the rare days when you find us stumbling on the roads down below, jumbled in our mind with hearts a little sore, slip in once again, perhaps at the end of the rainbow. Be the calm after the storm, the wind kissing our brow, the sunshine opening our eyes, to the Miracle that is our Life …

Lest We Forget.

With your passing, swiftly into Life Everlasting, we have gained a greater knowledge of Creation and a clearer understanding that Life itself is a Gift each one of us must Treasure. Forever, we will try to remember, what we have learned.

Precious Babies up above, Morgan Douglas and Kaleb Kevin, know always … that you are Loved.

Grandma

#5.   Andy

    Little scamp, spoiled brat, little boy blue, you choose. His name was Andy and he was all of two. The restaurant was busy over the lunch hour. Andy and his sitter were in a standoff. It was and stayed a battle of wills and I was an unwilling participant. I watched from across the table. One little boy and one determined sitter. She had just told him to look at her and obediently his head turned. Andy was so close I could have touched him had I reached across the table that separated us, so close and yet so far. Clearly I saw the sweet line of his plump, firm cheek, his determined little chin, the downcast curve of his full rosy lips. I sat spellbound as the sweep of thick lashes were raised to reveal the most beautiful blue eyes. These eyes were trained, unflinchingly, upon the face of his sitter. He was stubborn yes, that could not be denied, but I wondered in this instance, why? It was such a simple thing that she asked of him. Could it be the way that she asked, that created an obstacle too large to squash?

    His small head was held proud, upon little shoulders, bowed, beneath the weight of her censure. He was not going to say "Please" no matter the pressure she inflicted and that was great. He stood his ground against the harsh words that battered about his head. It was but conjecture on my part, only a feeling deep within my heart, that his wee heart was hurting. The eyes held all his thoughts, for anyone who cared to see, silently pleading that she would relent. His fisted hands sat still upon the table, never moving. He did not squirm, not once in his seat, nor did he kick his little feet under the table. I would have known.

    The only movement that I saw at all were the convulsive workings of his throat as he fought valiantly to keep back the tears that glistened and threatened to drop. I watched helplessly as he overcame the need to cry. So little, so young, so determined. He would not back down. He would not say Please! She asked him if he wanted to go to the car. Silently he shook his head, yes. He was only two what could we do? He was only a baby still and I so much wanted to gather him safely to me and hold him tight. I wished with all my heart to place a smile upon that dear sweet mouth. I wanted to tell him it didn't matter, that he did not have to say "please" and pour that ketchup over his chips.

Time and time again, bypassing the sitter, I tried to humor, cajole, tempt, play and practice my "please and thanks, all to no avail. I could not save him. He would not be saved. Then when I least expected it, I heard a small voice say, very quietly … "please". That was all that I needed. Quickly I ripped open the packet of ketchup and dumped it down by his fries.

He looked at me with a sparkle in his eyes. Short stubby fingers picked up the fry and dipped it in and gave it a try. His face split into an engaging grin and I smiled back at him. The fries dipped and dived and disappeared and they shyly, he offered one of those prized fries to me. The hell with my diet. I said, "Thank you Andy." He just looked at me and gave me another. We had no more trouble, but I'm still troubled. What was all that stubbornness about? Why dig in his heels when he could have dug in his fingers? There is only one thing certain. The little boy, a baby still, was pulling his own strings. He was living by his own agenda. He was fighting his own battles and winning, however imaginary these battles might have been. They were very real to him. He made me a believer in the strength of the human soul from one so young to one so old. (smc) **(Actual happening. I was there.)**

CHAPTER 29

I hope that you are still travelling with me on this bumpy winding road. Are the shocks in good repair? It's all about living the life you have been given and making it yours. Life is a circle of continuity. It will not be thwarted. Rather life must be engaged. You must taste it, feel it, and conquer it. It's a hell of a ride.

If I could I would give you the world, but it is not mine to give. The world and all that it has in store for you, is yours already. Do not stand on the sidelines. Life is the Pallet, you are the Artist! Do not hesitate or all will be lost. Begin to paint. Paint in large bold strokes with all the colour there is to see. Be creative, be imaginative, be strong, and take chances. Do not be left behind in the dust of the world's participants. Shout out loud and believe, "**this world is mine!**"

Capture the sunsets over a crystal clear lake. Mirror the mountains into it. Catch the evergreens along the shore. Grab a seagull flying high and place it in your sky. A baby round and rosy playing in the sand and a lonely old man with a fishing rod in his hand, these can be factored in. A faded row boat bobbing in the bay, a log cabin sitting on a jut of rocks, wet footprints on the dock, take note of these. Remember that treasures can be discovered in, out of the way places or just around the next corner. Be prepared to uncover all that you discover and it will enhance your life.

Do not miss a single one of the Miracles that come your way. Today is your day, always, into infinity.

Never give up on your dreams. Have you ever played the game of "**Baseball?**" You win some, you lose some, you tie some and all the while you are out of breath, you are energized, you are alive. **Life is also like that.** I personally love the game and played often when I was young. I've never lost my hankering for the sheer fun of it. I'm a senior now and I've

155

been advised not to play for reasons of my health. That makes me angry and sometimes anger is good because it is a motivator. Reasons given: my new hip does not allow me to run as I did when I was young. My balance is way off, like a ship caught in the wind, I list to the left. My eyes are not 20/20 and glasses are needed to keep me focused. But …. I'm up at Bat. The pitcher is on the mound warming up his arm. He is eyeing me up and down trying to psyche me out. I refuse to be intimidated. I'm holding firmly to my bat, elbows raised, knees bent. Will the pitch be slow or fast, high or low? What about the wicked curve ball? Iwill not swing until I know!

The ball leaves the pitchers' hand and I pay attention. Whatever is coming I am looking for the "sweet spot". The ball is closer now, whistling its way towards the plate. With muscles tense, eyeglasses on straight, calmly I wait. Timing is everything, **(always in all things)**. Ball and bat connect with the sweetest sound. The pitcher comes off the mound as I limp quickly towards first base. It's going to be close … this race. My feet touch the Bag. What a game! I'm huffing and puffing and my cheeks are red, but I'm 65 and still going strong. No way that is ever going to be wrong. I'm never giving up and just so you know, I expect the same of you!

So swing your bat and carry through, find the "sweet spot." Accept no limitations. This **Game of Life** is yours. Remember, you are an army of one setting out to discover, explore, overcome and rejoice in the Victory of you! Do not let life pass you by.

**You matter. You are the reason we are on
this page, right here, right now!**

There is a reason for this journey. There are nuggets of gold to be found on every pathway we follow and answers to all our questions from every person that we allow into our inner circle. They will in some way enhance the quality of our life.

Never doubt that there is much that we can learn from one another. Everything that we experience adds dimension to our life, shines light upon new horizons. We begin to set up borders that are acceptable to us and we walk away from actions not conducive to our health and happiness.

Every step taken brings us closer to the reality of self. Wisdom is what we have gained.

I state again, there is a purpose for this journey. I cannot stress this enough. Nothing we experience on life's roller coaster ….." **Is ever lost.**" Believe this.

We unknowingly file it away to be used for future reference. For every person we connect with, for every path we follow, for every decision made and every mistake we make, we learn, we grow, we become more confident. Each experience will be reflected in our future actions, as we filter in knowledge gained. We should never negate anyone or anything that impacts upon our lives, good or bad.

So ask yourself this question. Should we be building walls to surround us, to hide, safe, within their shadows? I believe that we would stagnate there!

Or should we be climbing every mountain there is to climb with our friend Courage at our side? Which answer will lead to a life worthwhile and well lived? There is only one healthy choice.

Imagine now, that Life as yours. Pretty incredible, isn't it!

Rejoice, be unafraid, there are really no mistakes we can make, that cannot turn into stumbling blocks of learning. With each step we come closer to our heart's desire and incredibly, our heart's desire can change with each lesson learned.

How we unravel the mystery of us, is our reward. You should find at the end of the journey, that what makes you happy, hopefully, is you, for you will discover, your own sweet Truth.

CHAPTER 30

So with this same knowledge in hand I ventured forth, stubborn, strong, courageous and ever hopeful. Certainly there would be someone who saw the beauty in me, someone who valued me just as I was, perfectly imperfect. I could not possibly be the only one who thought that I had worth. We would see.

To my surprise I met a young man that was not a love interest and who saw all too clearly the person that was me. Living alone with a large two bedroom apartment and holding down two jobs I came to the conclusion that I should get a roommate. I put an ad in the local newspaper and also on the site of Ontario Hydro. I wanted mature, male, preferably on shifts that went home when not working. Basically I wanted my cake and to eat it too. The phone rang and the first man I interviewed overwhelmed me with pure size 6'2" and massive frame. He was approximately my age, retired from work so I was told and he would be underfoot in my home, all of the time. This was not what I wanted. Did he not read the ad? I have never stepped back faster in my whole life. My mind was shouting ….. NO. No. No! I actually listened. We were not a match. He would have eaten up all my space and all the free air. I informed him that the room was gone.

I was more than ready to pack in this insane idea. What Had I been thinking? I loved my home, my space, my time. However, before I could recall my ad I received another call. Well perhaps I could give this one more try. If I still felt panicked and suffocated then that would be the end of it.

He came for an interview. I answered the knock on my door. We stood just for a fraction of a second taking in each other's measure and I immediately relaxed. There was no threat here. Before me stood my new tenant although he did not know it yet. He was tall and stood straight and strong and wore a jaunty relaxed smile. Just like that I knew. He turned out to be, over time, an answer to my prayers. We became true friends. He was happily married to the wife of his youth. He was very dedicated. He would be going home whenever he was off shift. We bumped along famously. I can honestly say that yes there was an initial attraction between the two of us but we knew, without words ever being spoken that would be as far as it went. We genuinely liked each other and in a short time respect followed. That was major for me.

We were confidents and shared our problems and stories and family interactions. He witnessed my struggles with relationships and he knew how very hard I worked at both of my jobs. He watched as I overcame every challenge I faced. He totally believed in me and I totally trusted him.

Life was good. Often I would wake up to breakfast he had made or enjoyed suppers he cooked after his shift at work. We were like family and yes the attraction was still there but not important. I was so very proud of both of us due to the fact that we never acted or wanted to act on that attraction. Best friends was something we both valued.

He was and in my mind still is, one of my very best, trusted and valued friends. I will always be grateful to him for discovering in me, someone worthy of his best efforts. We were together for perhaps two years and then something happened that might have changed, what we had achieved. I am not sure what exactly occurred but he left home unexpectedly, in the early hours after midnight, heading for here. I don't know why.

He must have been exhausted, still sleepy, when he made a stop at a garage prior to hitting the highway. The proprietor called the police believing he was intoxicated, or perhaps his manner had been a little gruff or to spell it out, he was in a mood. I will never know. He was flagged down by the OPP as he hit the highway and they booked him and his licence was taken away. When next I saw him he was rebellious, and he was angry. He had been put in the position of having to ask friends at work to give him a ride. It made his life harder and it hurt his pride. It was not surprising that his attitude changed.

I noticed small changes. We had always talked freely to one another about anything and everything. It was refreshing. One night as I was reading in bed he came to talk, leaning on the door frame. This was normal. He then moved to the end of the bed. He came closer and sat on the bed while we talked. This was unusual and I was feeling a little uncomfortable but by now we were dear friends. There was definitely no threat. Shortly after, he retired to get some sleep for an early morning shift. I realized later that perhaps he had been leading up to talking to me about what was bothering him. I wish that he had.

Another instance was that in our verbal tenant agreement he was to bring nobody else into my space. It was my home. He had never, not once, deviated from this request. One night coming home from work I walked into my home to face a complete stranger sitting at my dining room table with my tenant. The stranger was smoking. Smoking was definitely, not allowed in my home. I was surprised, I was tired and I was angry. It takes a lot to make me angry. What was going on? I don't think my tenant had ever seen me angry and I was angry with him. This had never happened before. I snatched the dirty dishes off the table and started washing them. He came up behind me and pecked the back of my neck, just as if he was making up for making me angry. This was simple affection but unusual.

We were never a couple and this was not the natural action of the man I knew. At this point I should have sat down with him and asked exactly what was wrong, what was happening with him and what I could do to help. I could have come up with solutions. That would have made me a much better friend. Instead I remained silent and a little confused.

A third incident occurred at the go station. It was a warm summer day. I had come to pick him up as he still did not have his licence back. The radio was on, the window was down and I was relaxed. I did not see him approaching. He came to my window, planted his hands on the car and leaned in to give me a kiss on the cheek.

It was very sweet, (if we had been a couple) and inappropriate as we were not. The funny thing was that in all honesty, there had been times when life was hard that a strong pair of arms to hold me would have been welcomed, but we never went there.

Did we have a possible problem? I understood that it was just a phase of rebellion due to circumstances, that had his priorities a little screwed up and yet he never really stepped out of line, not once. He was going through a rough time and his actions appeared to be escalating.

If we had taken the time to sit down together and get to the bottom of what was really wrong in his life, I may not have had to give up, such a beautiful friendship. However, I did not ask and he did not offer. Again, lost opportunities.

During this time frame my son and I were in the process of buying a home together. I had told my son that my tenant would be moving with us. My search area was one that I would make work for him in his present situation, close to transportation, access to shopping and restaurants and easy access for friends from work to pick him up.

Due to the current situation I felt I could not bring him with me when we moved.

It hurt me very much to break this friendship with my friend. I do miss him very much. This is another example of me not taking action. Time really doesn't stand still and opportunities we need, are lost, sometimes forever.

I totally take the blame for me not being the friend he needed at that time. With all my heart I hope that he found his way home and is happy.

Do you remember how I had been searching for someone who saw the beauty in me and valued who I was?

Well I found him and he turned out to be one of my very best friends. It is strange that he among the many male friends I met, was the one who really understood and valued who I was. The word **"Valued"** is important here. Hard to let go of that, because it's so very rare. Just so you know.

The scenarios that I have written are not always in their proper sequence. The people in my life are somewhat out of order on these pages. I do not believe it matters for they are forever in my Heart. The words run through my mind and drop unbidden upon the pages. Clarity comes in many forms at unexpected times and so I am comfortable with the results.

CHAPTER 31

I feel the time is right to let you know that I gave up on my search for a heart mate. Down through all my years of living and learning I grew stronger and found wisdom. I clearly saw who I was and loved who I saw.

I realized it was just possible that I was meant to travel the rest of my days separate and alone. I had not found a mate strong enough or spiritual enough or flexible enough to accept me just as I was. There was no one trusting enough to trust in who I had become.

I was not the young girl I had been. I no longer believed in fairy tales or make believe. I was now a realist and if I was the only one who believed in me, so be it! I had embraced my life.

I lived by my own rules. I trusted my own judgement. I was outspoken on matters of importance, positive, caring, and at peace with myself. That was the best part. I discovered I was happy. What more did I need?

I had left confusion and pain far behind and I wanted no part of that life anymore, for any reason. Not ever.

I accepted completely all the years of learning, all the self-doubts, the sorrows, the insecurities, the loneliness.

I chose to remember the pain that had started so long ago. It helped me to never accept that pain again, for any reason. I knew beyond a shadow of a doubt that I had needed to walk through that hell to get closer to the heaven I searched for.

I did not want to settle ever again, for less than what I gave. It would not happen. It became my mantra. My mind was at peace, my heart healed. All the scars that had mended it had made it strong.

My grandchildren brought me tremendous joy. I was no longer young and wondered why all the fuss about getting older. It was preferable to the alternative.

I was doing great without a mate. So as the days passed and contentment reigned and I lived my life my way, I felt that I had arrived. My children were grown, healthy and strong with children of their own. The dark days were gone. And then when you least expect it. When you stop wanting it, your world changes. The following story is one of my very favourites. **It was to be my happy ending!**

I still loved to dance so I had not given that up. Happy endorphins scattered about.

I had arranged to meet some friends, but first and most important I was going to a little church 45 minutes out of town to hear my two little granddaughters sing in public for the very first time. That was my priority. I was running behind schedule as per usual, (that has not changed) and so I left home not quite ready to go dancing. My hair was gathered back into a small pony and I was still wearing an old white top that I now used for pj's. Really this outfit was not acceptable, definitely not special. I was only half ready. I obviously was beyond caring.

On the return journey I did not have time to go home and change. So there I was in all my natural glory at the dance. It just does not get any better than that. Well I had always been a risk taker and the right attitude can pretty much take you anywhere. I could handle this. In I walked.

At one point I was sitting quietly at our table while my friends were up dancing. As I searched the room for them, my eyes wandered to the far side of the room. There across the vast expanse of dance floor was a very exceptional looking man. He was so very handsome and I had never seen him before. Curious, I decided to get a closer look and so I joined my friends on the floor. Holy cow, my sight was not faulty. There he sat totally relaxed with a mixed group of male and female. Questions roared through my head. Was he with someone, was he available?

(I would never interfere with a couple, not for anything.)

At the end of the song, feeling brave for some unknown reason I approached the stranger. Our conversation went something like this. Touching his shoulder to get his attention I asked, "Are you here with someone?' His immediate response was, "yes, with him," as he indicated the man beside him. The term "gay" jumped into my brain. "Oh! I'm sorry." I exclaimed and stepped quickly away. He reached out and grabbed my hand and pulled me back. He was laughing. It turns out he was not gay but knew exactly what I had been thinking. Point one, he had a sense of humor and was an original. Yes he wanted to dance and said it had been a long time. He was fit, well dressed and mimicked every dance move I made. It was hilarious fun and I was laughing and smiling the whole time. He was a quick study. The risk of rejection had been worth the effort.

That was in November 2007. We danced only three dances all of them fast.

Note: *As you know by now my mind works in weird and wonderful ways that only I completely understand.*

I felt strongly that I should not monopolize him, it would not be fair to the other girls there. I thanked him for the dances and left him free to roam. We never exchanged names or numbers. Was this to be a one time interaction?

I admit freely that I thought about this stranger I had met quite often after that, but as fate would have it, circumstance, a busy life, family and friends kept me away from that dance for quite a few months. Would he be there when I went back, was a question that I quietly asked myself? Would I even recognize him if he was there? After six months I really could not remember what he looked like. His face was but a shadow in my mind.

In May 2008, six months after our initial meeting, I made it back to that particular location for dancing. I was having a good time, dancing up a storm. As I returned to our table my friend pointed to a man sitting beside her and said, "I believe you know this man."

Startled because he was totally unfamiliar to me I looked more closely and said doubtfully, "I'm sorry, I do not think that we have ever met." I totally believed that. As the story progressed I learned that they had been talking and she pointed to me on the dance floor and said, that is my friend out there. After watching for a few minutes he said, "I think I know her. Did she not have" he hesitated, "blonde hair?"

My friend laughed and said, "Don't you mean white?" "Yes, that's it. Her hair was white." To clarify the subject for him, he was told that I usually wore wigs of different colours and styles, when I went out dancing.

I was still not clueing in to the fact that we had met and I had not been there for this conversation. He asked me to dance and on the dance floor he did exactly what he had done before, he mimicked my every move, and then he smiled and then I knew.

He had put on thirty wholesome pounds since our first meeting and his face was more round and physically he loomed larger. The amazing thing about that second meeting was that he told me every single detail about our original meeting down to what we said, how we danced, what I was wearing and how my hair was not done. I found that remarkable.

I could flirt with the best of them and clown around and have fun, but if I was truly attracted to someone I reverted back to the real me. I had always been a shy, quiet, standing at the back of the room kind of gal. With him I retreated. My friend on the other hand had no such qualms.

Push, push, shove and demand. Well she gave us a much needed push or once again we might have parted never to meet again. She went overboard and practically forced him to ask for my phone number. I was totally embarrassed. I could have swatted her but realized later I was glad I hadn't.

He by now had my first name. We were progressing. When we were leaving he and his friend walked out with us and as fate would have it our vehicles were parked side by side. Coincidence? For future reference his initials were, (DRH). He and I continued to talk and he surprised me by asking if I would like to go to brunch with him and his friend at the Casino on Sunday. I believe he was playing the friend card for safety sake, but he did not seem to be wasting any time. It was a long weekend in May and so I said yes, I would like to go.

It was now Friday. Just two days to wait. I admit I was rather excited but nervous. I had not been dating for a long time.

On Saturday I was relaxing in my room reading a great book when the phone rang. Irritated, I looked at the screen and saw (DR _H_____). Since when did doctors call their patients, especially on the weekend? It must be a wrong number and I let it slip into voice mail.

When I put my book down I remembered the phone had rang and I checked to see if a message had been left. It was him! No doctor had called. He went by his second name and I had no idea what the D stood for. Funny that I had thought it was a doctor. It appeared that he was stepping out of his comfort zone.

The message, "Was I free and would I like to go to the show tonight?" Nervous but intrigued I agreed. To this day neither one of us can remember what show we saw. We just seemed to click.

The long and short of it was that we started dating. Our natures were totally opposites.

He was immaculate, organized, ran a tight ship, had to have a plan, had a rotation system for every object in his home.

So far he has not rotated me. I think the term is "regimented, methodical." Everything he does is done with excellence but taken one step at a time. He is sweet and funny.

I on the other hand was a messy, spontaneous, whirlwind, more emotional than logical, who flew mostly by the seat of my pants.

I could handle many projects and juggle them all at the same time with great results. In so many ways we were miles apart.

He rotated around facts and I rotated around heart.

The wonderful thing about our differences were, as time passed I came to love being able to find my keys and knowing exactly where the scissors were and never running out of everything. I could get used to this.

He learned to relax a little more and expect the unexpected and roll with the changes.

We were good for one another in so many ways that our differences made no difference.

He is a team player and I was in need of that. He loved his kids and that was major for me.

He embraced with love, my whole family and that took a lot of embracing. My family is huge.

It was effortless for him. He speaks randomly to perfect strangers about his five children. He pointed out to me that each one of them fit in age and could easily have been ours from the start.

He tries hard not to show his Heart but it just shines through, especially when he holds the grandchildren in his arms.

My family loves him and so do I. He is not easy but when he is being good he is a hell of a great guy. Just so you know.

A simple example of his organization and rotation skills and one of my sweetest memories of us is this. In the beginning everything is new. Right?

We were making supper one night at his place and I was setting the table and setting out condiments. "What salad dressing do you want" I asked? "The next one", he answered.

"From which end" I replied. "The right side" he stated.

Question from me! What if you don't feel like the next one" I said with a smile, and he answered as if I were serious, **"I can be Flexible!"**

The sweet part of this story is that he truly believes he is flexible. We are still working on that one.

Spring is here and May is just around the corner and we have been together for seven really memorable years.

Like all relationships we have mountains to climb and valleys to rest in and a great deal of compromise going on. We try to be fair. We are on the same team but sometimes our outlook is off kilter.

It's a juggling act and neither one of us is ready to drop the ball. It takes a lot of strength, patience and wisdom to keep that ball in the air, but we both love the game of baseball, so there is a chance that we can pull this off.

Nowadays I move on a day to day basis, knowing nothing in this world of ours, is guaranteed.

My eyes are wide open and I am holding back a piece of my heart, just in case, for safety's sake. **Is this my happy ending?** Well the jury is still out on this particular case, but for now I am happy.

Life makes us no promises. It's often contradictory to what we believe will make us happy, so I go forward, without hesitation, wondering, waiting.

Is this man another stepping stone or the foundation of happily ever after?

Regardless of the outcome I will never lose sight of the person that I have become, while always remembering this most amazing journey that I did not want to make.

CHAPTER 32

Counting my Blessings:

Hello, good morning, I could not sleep. This drives me crazy! My mind decided it was in a spin cycle and pulled me in. The quiet of my night was disturbed by my thoughts. Oh darn. It's 5:56 am on a Saturday. I wander down the hallway of my home in search of my computer, or pen and paper or whatever. It seems that sleep once again, was not essential. Who Knew?

I am hopeful that all those crazy thoughts I have been thinking can be reproduced upon this page. For some reason in the middle of my night, I am thinking about my grandchildren. DRH and I together have five children and ten grandchildren.

They are all so beautifully perfect each in their own special way.

Starting with the older ones, I was thinking about a bright shining star, always in your face and talking a mile a minute with this great big dazzling smile. She is tremendously intelligent and yet feels no need to dwell upon it. She prefers to act flakey. She embraces her immediate world which is high school, with confidence. Her teachers are not sure what to make of her and I believe that is her whole point.

Another child is quiet and introspective and sweet and adorable yet holds back a little on her own potential, not quite sure of her direction, making no definite decisions as she surveys her world and her place in it. I talk to these sisters, so different and yet much the same, but usually I just sit and listen to them talk and I hear what they say. I understand that each in her own way has a handle on who they are and what they believe. I see their strength and their beauty and I rejoice.

Another child is tall and slim and very beautiful and yet in need of something she has yet to find within herself, confidence. Her potential is great and I believe she can accomplish most anything as soon as she finds her feet.

Another little girl, her sister has a totally different personality and walks fearlessly into her life. They are very protective of one another and with love balance out their world. I love this bond. These two are not as chatty as the others, a little hesitant, a little shy and totally loveable.

The next in line is a little darling of eight. She has two sets of parents and a huge heart and her life is often in turmoil. She is a brave little girl who since the age of three has tried to juggle the constants in her life. The weight of this is much too heavy for her tiny shoulders and her searching heart.

She was recently diagnosed with an ailment I have never heard of. In all honesty I was a basket case. Bottom line for me now is to never place restrictions on the true potential of any child. Each child is born with a unique heart and soul and Miracles are all around us. Build on the positives and let love flow. When she runs into my arms, I bring her home.

We have only two grandsons. They are both far away out west. We have a total of four precious grandkids out there for that is where three of our children reside. We see them seldom and love them always.

The oldest is 16 and when we saw them last Thanksgiving he told us he wanted to be an engineer. Wow. So young to make such a statement and it was completely unexpected.

Will he make it? Again we do not know but no restrictions are allowed. We are very proud of him and we notice that the grandkids are growing up so fast, while DRH and I are slowing down.

Our other grandson is going to be a total of two this May. From the moment he was born he was bright eyed, curiously aware and a source of pure joy.

His beautiful older sister is much the same with a gentle and loving heart, a happy smile and a head full of bouncing curls. She is going on four.

Back home there is her cousin who is just four months younger, three still, a sweet little darling who melts into your arms and into your heart.

How could two grandparents ever be as fortunate as we?

Well, just last summer we got a bonus, perhaps our last grandchild who will be one this summer. She is absolutely perfect in every single way.

As grandparents, we live for pictures.

These grandchildren are my greatest joy. There is not a thing that I have done in my life to be worthy of such happiness and yet I will be eternally grateful for the Gift of each one of them.

Being their grandmother has been the best job that I have ever had. They happened at a time, when I had time. It's about time. Know that time is of the essence and treasure it always. Do not let it slip away.

CHAPTER 33

God made each one of us as a unique entity. There is no one anywhere quite like us. We should rejoice in this fact. We each react if only fractionally, a tad differently, to the same outside interactions. I might hear a bird song at dawn and find it beautiful and you might throw a pillow over your head to drown out what you perceive as noise.

Our differences do not matter in the great scheme of things. When I was young I was told that we need contrasts in all things or they would be of no value to us. They would hold no meaning.

How would we differentiate between good and evil if we had no experience of one of those elements? How does water feel as compared to air? We appreciate warmth and relate it to summer because if you live here the winters are brutally cold. Of course I have friends that prefer the cold. I don't get it and yet though we differ in thoughts and minds and hearts at times, we are still the best of friends.

I might look frumpy in mismatched colours and styles that I love and you might be perfectly put together in designer duds. I respect your right to be happy with your choices and I know that usually I am happy with the choices that I make. We all can learn from one another or at least we should try.

The world, minute by minute is becoming so much smaller than ever before. Countries that we may never have heard of, could be knocking at our door. Are we going to be ready for that?

Will the world be able to adjust to our differences and live in harmony with one another? This is a huge question. Somewhere there is an answer. We must believe in this.

With Faith I walk these roads down below trying to hold onto a sense of self. I will never be perfect but I will remain, perfect in my imperfections.

I will always do the best I can with the talents that I have been blessed with and I can honestly say, that I have never been bored. How amazing is that? How could I possibly be when all the wonders of this world surround me?

Although we have never met, know that you are one of those wonders. By your mere existence, by what you do and what you accomplish, you will impact my world. We all matter, no matter what. Never forget that. Embrace every single moment to give you the strength to embrace the next. The journey that you make and how you make it, is what should be important to you. Who am I really? The answer to that question will bring clarity to your life. Remember nobody else needs to know how wonderful you really are, so embrace your life and with wonder continue the journey.

When the curtain falls upon my last days here upon this earth I know that I will carry gently the memory of our children and grandchildren with me to share with my loved ones who have gone on before. There is more to my life than the here and now and yet this frail existence is but a prelude to possibilities, new adventures and a happiness far greater than we can ever imagine.

CHAPTER 34

The Patchwork Quilt

Looking back thru the years it seems that I had been like a tiny bud, tightly closed, surrounded with protective petals like walls to keep me safe. I had been asleep. One morning in the warmth of the sun's rays, my petals opened one by one by one and I awakened into my first day of being totally alone, in the real world, to make my own way.

Eventually the beauty that lay within, emerged, energized and exploded as this great adventure continued. It was all new to me. It did not seem to matter how humble my beginnings, what knowledge I would gain, how strong or frail I was. Once awakened and forced to leave my sheltered life, the pathways I found to follow, led me on a journey of discovery that has blown the cobwebs from my mind.

In time I discovered that I exist for this. I had no compass to guide me on this unknown journey. I had no expectations of what wonders I might find or how scary it might be. Like thistle down, the breezes carried me to new discoveries and a world that could be construed, as upside down. I found that it all depended on my point of view and that point of view was all up to me. Freedom of Choice. Free Agency. What will my new life be? Let's see.

I found myself in places that I did not wish to go and yet I met there, so many people that I was meant to know, as I searched for my new reality. With each uncertain step I took I was challenged and rose to the challenge. What else could I do? Choices were all around me and all those choices were mine. What would the results be, good, bad, happy sad? I would soon see that life, was a mixed bag of reality.

My life became a patchwork quilt and not all the patches were made of spun gold or silken threads.

Some of the patches were in shades of brown like the rich warm earth. **(Balance)** Some patches were majestic and pure as snow topped mountains caught in the rays of the morning sun. **(Promise)** Some patches were powerful and based on continuity, like the mighty oceans, which left me **(Grounded).** Other patches were a combination of muted colours like scattered autumn leaves. **(Renewal)** There were patches that blended and flowed together like a cold mountain stream, clear and clean, tumbling over granite rock into a rainbow waterfall. **(Powerful).** All these patches were splattered with the memory of all the people that I chose to know. Those people enriched my life and helped me to learn and to grow strong. The quilt would not be complete, without those.

My life became like that quilt, unexpected, challenging, and full of wonder. There was a whole world out there that I knew nothing about. As my path wandered to places unknown with hills to climb and meadows gentle, I found at last, **my own rhythm**. I made my own decisions and learned from my own mistakes. Bravely I uncovered someone that I might never have known and I rejoiced in the person that I had found. I had survived. I could stand proud.

Moments in time:

I stood rocking a little boy in my arms. He was missing his mom. Tears were running down his cheeks. I carried him to the patio door and pointing my finger I whispered, **"Look".** The tears stopped as we watched rain falling on towering evergreens and pointing higher we saw the sun, battling to break through the clouds. The day was all confused.

Silently, together, we watched fat raindrops sliding along needles, green and slippery and sharp. A single drop was caught and held, just for an instant within a sunbeam, before it plopped to the sodden earth below. He looked at me and I at him and within that moment, he surprised me with a grin!

Have you ever stood in awe and watched the sun rise into a clear morning sky, as it pushes gently against the night. There is no stopping the earth's rotation. This is known as "Dawn Awakening."

Tiny Gifts of sweet delight are all around us. Take a moment to experience, **"Pure Beauty."** What will you do with this new day? It's Gods' Gift to you. The page is clean, crisp and all yours. Write your own story. Embrace the opportunity. You are its' Author. The Gifts that surround us will not be found unless we ourselves, **"Stop to breathe."** That breath and the next and the next are all precious gifts. We need to remember this.

Time stands still just for a second and then it is gone, lost forever. It does not wait for you or I. Time matters. This moment and all the moments we are allowed, fill them to overflowing with all the knowledge and sweetness and love that you have found.

Know that goodness is possible within each one of us. Do not look back upon your past, but rather take with you only moments to treasure from days gone by and step forward without fear. Make this world your own. The possibilities are endless.

Weave, sew, knit, gather, collect and frame your masterpiece, it is after all, your life. Know that every stitch you stitch, you earned! Leave nothing out. It all adds up to a beautiful you. Look upon your patchwork quilt and with wonder, acknowledge and give thanks to who you have become.

You have always mattered. Never doubt that.

Know also that it does not matter nor should it, what the world sees. Remember, they do not know you. This Truth is vital. It matters only what you know to be true, about you, what you have learned, what you believe and what you yourself have achieved. **The only true picture of you, is yours!** You need to remember this.

The world can be a wonderful place to live your life, but the world is made up of people and people, get lost. Be grateful that you are no longer one of them! As it is written, "To thine own self be true." Others are still on the journey for their own Patch Work Quilt. Allow them to discover their own truth, like you did. It's the only way to happiness.

CHAPTER 35

<u>As for me and my journey.</u>

The storm tossed sea is releasing me. The huge waves lift and carry me steadily towards the Shallows.

The undertow, reluctantly lets go. I'm walking free. The distant shore is not so distant anymore.

The sun sparkles on waters blue. My patch work quilt beckon's from the shore in a melody of rainbow colours and a sweet harmony of history. That history is mine. Memories surround me, uplift me.

Surprisingly, I feel energized and I find myself smiling. I cannot stop. Why did I take so long, before I understood ... **My Life?**

My journey has brought me to **"Safe Harbour home."**

The torch I have been carrying to light my path, I now hand over to you, my fellow traveller.

Hold it high that Its' light might shine and chase away your Shadows. Perhaps soon you will clearly see, your own sweet destiny.

I say **"Goodbye"** to you, as my journey takes another turn. Know that you are not forgotten. Remember always that you matter!

To the Strangers that became my friends and more, to the family and friends I loved before, to the grandchildren my heart adores, with love and sweet humility, I thank you.

Life is an incredible journey of self-discovery. I wish for all of you the Courage and Sweetness of discovering yours.

<u>The End…But Not Really</u>

ABOUT THE AUTHOR

Alberta Mann is not a figment of the imagination. She had the most profound effect on this author. She is very strong willed, funny, compassionate, and brave. Her faith is strong and her outlook on the world, unique. She often sees that which others fail to see. She is an avid reader, mostly regency romances (Georgette Heyer) and mystery suspense (Clive Cussler), for example.

The author has been writing for three decades with never an impulse to publish. Now retired, she has the time. This is her first book. The words fall quietly upon a blank page, and they tell a story that is unlike what the author started out to say. It has always been that way. It's magical! She does not change it.

If you can look upon a sunset sinking into the sea and see ultimate beauty, if you love the rustle of leaves under your feet and the wind talking to the trees, you are one with her.

Her grandchildren leave her speechless. They are priceless!

From a heart of gold, which has been battered and bruised, rises in beauty a spirit still intact and forever positive. She believes always in the power of love and the power of self.

Truth will always be the strongest tool she has. It's her reality. It is her strength.

Printed in the United States
By Bookmasters